The Tales of
Tinker Bell

The Tales of Tinker Bell

TINKER BELL TAKES CHARGE
WRITTEN BY GAIL HERMAN

THE TROUBLE WITH TINK
WRITTEN BY KIKI THORPE

A MASTERPIECE FOR BESS
WRITTEN BY LARA BERGEN

HarperCollins *Children's Books*

This edition first published in Great Britain in 2007
by HarperCollins Children's Books.
HarperCollins Children's Books is a division of
HarperCollins Publishers,
77 - 85 Fulham Palace Road, Hammersmith, London, W6 8JB.

The HarperCollins Children's Books website is:
www.harpercollinschildrensbooks.co.uk

978-0-00-725410-1
0-00-725410-5

1 3 5 7 9 10 8 6 4 2

Printed and bound in the UK

Visit disneyfairies.com

This book is proudly printed on paper which contains wood
from well managed forests, certified in accordance with
the rules of the Forest Stewardship Council.
For more information about FSC,
please visit www.fsc-uk.org

Mixed Sources
Product group from well-managed
forests and other controlled sources
www.fsc.org Cert no. SW-COC-1806
© 1996 Forest Stewardship Council

All About Fairies

IF YOU HEAD toward the second star on your right and fly straight on till morning, you'll come to Never Land, a magical island where mermaids play and children never grow up.

When you arrive, you might hear something like the tinkling of little bells. Follow that sound and you'll find Pixie Hollow, the secret heart of Never Land.

A great old maple tree grows in Pixie

Hollow, and in it live hundreds of fairies and sparrow men. Some of them can do water magic, others can fly like the wind, and still others can speak to animals. You see, Pixie Hollow is the Never fairies' kingdom, and each fairy who lives there has a special, extraordinary talent.

Not far from the Home Tree, nestled in the branches of a hawthorn, is Mother Dove, the most magical creature of all. She sits on her egg, watching over the fairies, who in turn watch over her. For as long as Mother Dove's egg stays well and whole, no one in Never Land will ever grow old.

Once, Mother Dove's egg *was* broken. But we are not telling the story of the egg here. Now it is time for Tinker Bell's tale...

Tinker Bell
Takes
Charge

1

IT WAS A MILD, sunny day in Pixie Hollow – a perfect sort of a day. Little white clouds scampered across a dazzling blue sky. A soft breeze rustled the leaves of the Home Tree, the great ageless maple where the Never fairies lived.

Although it was a perfect day, Tinker Bell was not in her usual high spirits. Something was bothering her, but she could not figure out what it was. She wasn't sick. She wasn't sad. It was more like she had an itch that she couldn't find, let alone scratch.

Just that morning, she had caught sight of her face in the polished walls of the Home Tree's lobby. She'd noticed her slumped shoulders and the frown on her face. Even her ponytail drooped.

This troublesome feeling was on her mind now as she flew toward her bedroom, which was high in the branches of the Home Tree. She needed to change her shoes before she could go back to her workshop. The ones she was wearing had gotten soaked on a visit to Thistle's strawberry patch. Thistle, a garden-talent fairy, had asked Tink to look at a garden hoe that needed fixing. It had been left on the damp ground among the strawberries, and the blade had rusted through. It would have to be replaced. *But it will be easy to fix,* Tink thought.

She headed up through the trunk of the Home Tree. The trunk split into branches. She turned right, then left, then left again, winding upward. The corridor narrowed as the tree's limbs tapered.

Tink's bedroom was at the end of one of the topmost branches. When the hallway was so tight that her head nearly grazed the ceiling, she reached the door to her room.

As soon as she was inside, her spirits lifted a bit. Tink loved her room. Everything in it reflected her talent and personality. There was her beloved bed, which was made from a pirate's metal loaf pan. There were the lampshades made from old colanders. Even the chair she was sitting on was special. The back of it was made from a serving platter, the seat was a frying pan, and the legs were made from old serving spoons.

At one point or another, Tink had repaired the frying pan, the platter, and each of the spoons. Some she had repaired more than once. But eventually, pans and spoons wore out. Although Tink thought anything broken could be fixed, the kitchen-talent fairies didn't always agree. Sometimes they threw their worn-out pots and platters away.

Tink felt a special connection with every pot and pan she'd ever fixed. She couldn't bear to see any of them on the scrap-metal heap. So when the kitchen-talent fairies had thrown out the pan, the platter, and the spoons, she'd rescued them and brought them back to her workshop. With a lot of thought and a few pinches of fairy dust, she'd turned them into a chair.

Tink thought about the frying-pan chair as she closed the door to her room and flew back down through the Home Tree. What a wonderful challenge it had been to make. Not like fixing Thistle's silly rusted hoe. There was nothing hard about replacing a hoe blade. No challenge at all.

Suddenly Tink stopped in her tracks.

"That's it!" she said aloud. "That is what's bothering me! No challenge!"

Tink was one of the best pots-and-pans-talent fairies in all of Pixie Hollow. Her joy came from fixing things. She liked a challenging problem more than almost anything.

But for weeks now, every job Tink had been given had been as easy as gooseberry pie. No pots that wouldn't boil water. No colanders that refused to drain. No pans that were more hole than pan. Just "fix this little hole, fix that little hole." Boring, boring, boring.

But at least now I know what's wrong, Tink thought. *What I need is a problem to solve! A big one!*

"Tink!" A voice behind her interrupted her thoughts. Tink turned. Her good friend Rani, a water-talent fairy, was hurrying toward her.

Being the only fairy without wings,

Rani could not fly. So Tink gently landed on the moss carpet in the Home Tree's hallway. She waited until Rani caught up.

"Where are you going?" Rani asked.

"I was just on my way back to my workshop," Tink replied. "Why do you – "

"Ask?" said Rani. She had a habit of finishing everyone's sentences. "No big reason. I just thought maybe we could play a game of – "

But Rani never got to finish. At that moment, she was interrupted by a tremendous crash. Both fairies heard branches cracking and snapping near the top of the Home Tree.

In the next instant, there was a *thud* that shook the tree to its very roots.

Tink and Rani nearly lost their balance. From the nearby tearoom came the sound of dishes falling and shattering.

Then there was silence.

Tink and Rani stared at each other.

"Did the moon just fall out of the sky?" Rani whispered in awe.

"Maybe it was a branch falling from another tree," said Tink. But even as she spoke, she knew that wasn't it. The sound had been made by something very heavy and solid. And it had landed quite close by.

"Maybe a great big bird just came in for a landing," said Rani.

"Maybe," said Tink. But that didn't seem right either.

The two fairies listened carefully. After a long moment Tink took a deep breath and straightened her shoulders. "We've got to go and see – "

"What it is. If you say so," said Rani. She dabbed her forehead with a leafkerchief and attempted to smile bravely. Though they were both nervous, it was a lot easier to see it on Rani. She was the most watery of all the water- talent fairies. At the moment, her forehead was beaded with sweat.

The two fairies headed back toward the front entrance of the Home Tree. Tink walked so that she wouldn't get too far ahead of Rani. Brave as she was, even Tink didn't want to go outside alone. Together they hurried past the tearoom, down the corridor, through the lobby, and out the knothole door.

When Tink stepped into the

sunlight, she stopped cold and gasped. Rani, who was right on Tink's heels, crashed into her.

Rani peeked over Tink's shoulder. She gasped, too.

"*What* is *that?*" she whispered.

2

RIGHT IN FRONT of them was a huge, menacing-looking black ball. It was taller than two fairies put together and just as wide. It had landed right in the middle of the Home Tree's courtyard.

A large crack ran through the courtyard where it had smashed down. Several toadstool chairs had been damaged or squashed completely. The ground around the ball was covered with the splintered remains of branches and twigs.

Tink's mind reeled. The courtyard was a very special place for the fairies. Many of their most important meetings and celebrations were held there. Not to mention, the fairies had to fly through it to reach the Home Tree's knothole door.

Whenever Tink saw the courtyard, she felt that she was home. It always seemed to say, "Welcome. The Home Tree waits to embrace you." Now the sight of the damaged courtyard made her heart ache.

A large crowd of fairies had gathered around the ball. Clarion, the fairy queen, stepped forward.

"Is everyone all right?" she asked. Her voice was tense with worry. "Is anyone hurt?"

Noses and wings were quickly counted, amid a buzz of concern. Incredibly, every fairy in the Home Tree had escaped harm.

The queen sighed with relief. She looked around the crowd. "Terence, Spring, Jerome, Rosetta, Luna," she said.

Her voice had regained its normal regal tone. The fairies and sparrow men sprang to attention. "Fly to the top of the tree and see what damage has been done. Please report back at once."

With Terence, a fairy-dust-talent sparrow man, in the lead, the group took off.

When they had gone, a scullery-talent fairy tiptoed up to the great ball. She raised her hand as if to touch its rough surface. But at the last second she pulled her hand back. "Do you think it might be alive?" she whispered.

All at once, the fairies nearest to the ball hopped back a couple of steps.

"What's it made of?" asked Dulcie, a baking-talent fairy.

The fairies around her shook their

heads, muttering, "Don't know."

"Maybe it's a big rock," said Angus, a pots-and-pans-talent sparrow man. "Though I've certainly never seen a rock this round before."

"Maybe it's a giant black pearl," said Rani. "Though I've never seen a pearl this big."

Tink shook her head. "No," she said. "It would be shiny if it were a pearl."

Dulcie flew hesitantly up to it. She gave it a small rap with her knuckles. "Ow!" she said. "It's hard!" She blew on her hand. "And it's hot!" she added.

Tink didn't like to stand around. And she had stood around long enough. Bravely, she marched up to the ball and gave it a good hard smack.

"It's iron," she said. She shook her hand to cool it off from the hot metal. "Good old-fashioned Never iron."

Several fairies frowned. "Iron is really heavy," Dulcie said worriedly.

"It's going to be hard to move," said Rani. She started to cry.

"We should try to find out where it came from," the queen told them. "That might help us figure out how to get rid of it."

Her suggestion was greeted with enthusiasm. "Let's take a good look at it," said Rani. She wiped the tears from her eyes.

The fairies all moved in closer. They circled the ball. Some fairies flew around the top. Others bent down low to look at the part that touched the ground.

"Hold on!" said Tink. She hovered like a hummingbird near the very top of the ball. "I see something."

Other fairies flew over to join her. "You're right," said Lily, a garden-talent fairy. "It's some kind of a mark."

Angus nodded. "It's almost like a – "

"A hook!" Tink shouted in triumph. "It's a mark that looks like a hook! And you know what that means."

"Captain Hook!" cried several fairies.

"Of course. Why didn't I realise it before? It's a cannonball!" Tink declared.

Tink had seen plenty of cannonballs back in the days when she had spent all her time with Peter Pan. But she had never before seen a cannonball in Pixie Hollow. Hook and his pirates never came to this part of Never Land's forest. And the fairies tried to avoid the pirates as much as they could.

Just then, they heard a muffled boom from the direction of Pirate Cove. Several fairies jumped.

"Cannon fire," said Queen Clarion. "Captain Hook must be after Peter Pan again."

The others knew what she meant. On Never Land, there was an on-and-off battle between Hook and his pirates and Peter and the Lost Boys. On certain quiet nights, when the wind was just right, the fairies could hear Pan and Hook's swords clashing in the distance.

"Hmm," said Tink with a worried

little frown. Peter Pan was a friend of Tink's. Though she rarely saw him anymore, she knew him better than any of the other fairies did. She didn't like to think of Captain Hook firing cannonballs at Peter.

But Peter is too quick and too clever to get hit by a cannonball, Tink assured herself.

There was another muffled boom, followed by a whizzing sound.

"Everyone, duck!" said the queen.

The fairies all dashed for cover in the roots of the Home Tree. Something flew through the air high over their heads. It landed in the nearby forest with a tremendous thud.

"The fairy circle!" cried Dulcie. She hurried out from behind a root.

"What if it landed there?"

"What about Mother Dove?" Rani said, almost in a whisper. "What if it hit her hawthorn tree?"

The fairies looked at each other in stricken silence. Mother Dove was the closest thing to pure goodness in all of Never Land. She was the source of all the fairies' magic. They had almost lost her once, when a hurricane hit Never Land. The thought of losing her again was too dreadful to bear.

In a tense voice, Queen Clarion told several fast-flying fairies to fly to the hawthorn and check on Mother Dove. They zipped off in a blur.

Moments later, the fast fliers were back.

"Mother Dove is fine," a fast-flying

sparrow man reported. "Not one feather ruffled. And the fairy circle is undamaged."

The fairies let out a collective sigh of relief.

Tink glared at the big black cannonball in the courtyard. "How dare those pirates!" she exclaimed. "How could they be so careless? I say – "

But before she could say more, Spring, a message-talent fairy, came speeding up to her. She had a grim look on her face.

"Tink," she said. "I've just been to the top of the Home Tree. I think you'd better come with me."

3

WHAT NOW? Tink wondered. *And what does it have to do with me?*

Maybe something metal has broken, and they need me to fix it, Tink mused. *But why right at this moment?*

She followed the messenger into the Home Tree. They passed through the main corridor, where paintings representing each different Never fairy talent hung on the walls. Tink saw that most of the paintings were crooked. Some had even fallen to the floor. She stopped and straightened the painting of a dented stewpot, which was the symbol for the pots-and-pans talent.

Up through the branches they went. They turned right, then left, then left again. Finally, they came to the corridor that led to Tink's room. Tink saw her friend Terence waiting for her. Terence had been in the group the queen had sent to check the damage to the tree. He looked upset.

"Tink," he said, "I hardly know how to tell you this. Your bedroom – "

Her beloved bedroom! Tink didn't even wait for him to finish his sentence. She zoomed down the corridor to the end of the branch where her room sat. What would she find? she wondered. Would it be a horrible mess? Would her loaf-pan bed be overturned, or even dented? It was not a pleasant thought.

When she reached the tip of the branch, she stopped cold.

Her room wasn't a mess. Her room

wasn't there at all.

Tinker Bell hovered, staring. The walls, the ceiling, and everything in the room had disappeared. All that remained was the floor and the jagged edges of the broken walls.

She looked up past the hole where her ceiling should have been. The surrounding branches had a few broken twigs. But the other fairies' rooms were still there. The cannonball had hit Tink's room, and Tink's alone.

Tink felt faint. She sat down cross-legged on the floor.

How could my room just be... gone? she thought. *Where will I sleep? Where will I keep my clothes and other things? Where are my clothes and other things?*

More fairies began to arrive to

see what had happened.

"Oh, Tink," said her friend Beck. "It's awful!"

"I can't believe it," said Prilla. "Your bed is gone. And it was such a great bed."

Tink stood up. She didn't want the other fairies to feel sorry for her. She took a deep breath. "We'll just rebuild it," she said. She sounded calmer than she felt. "And it will be an even better room than before."

"We'll all help you," said Terence. The others nodded in agreement.

Suddenly Tink felt angry. After all, no one would have to rebuild anything if it weren't for the cannonball. Her hands balled into tiny fists thinking about it.

"And in the meantime," she said

fiercely, "we're going to get that horrid cannonball out of our courtyard. What do you say, fairies?"

"Yes!" they all cried. "Let's do it!" With Tink in the lead, the fairies went back to the courtyard. The most obvious thing was to try pushing the cannonball, Tink decided. "If a lot of us get behind it and fly as hard as we can, maybe we can roll it out of the courtyard," she said.

"Let's move every little twig out of its path. That way it won't get stuck on anything," said Beck.

The cleaning-talent fairies grabbed their brooms and swept up all the splinters. Other fairies helped by moving the pieces of the squashed mushroom chairs.

"All right," said Tink. "Let's get into pushing formation."

Several fairies arranged themselves behind the ball. The strongest ones hovered close to the bottom. The weaker ones stayed near the top.

"One, two, three… *shove!*" shouted Tink.

The fairies beat their wings madly. They heaved against the ball as hard as they could.

After a moment, they stopped. Several fairies leaned against the ball, panting.

"I think it moved a tiny, tiny bit," said Prilla, who was inclined to see the best in all situations.

"It didn't move an inch," said Angus, who was not.

"Let's give it another try," said Tink.

They rearranged themselves. Now the strongest fairies went to the top of the ball. The weaker ones went to the bottom.

"One, two, three... *shove!*" Tink cried again.

The fairies used every ounce of strength they had. At last they stopped. Their wings were quivering with exhaustion.

"Nothing," said Angus.

Indeed, the ball had not moved, not a hair.

Tink sighed. "Well, I guess that's not going to work," she said. "But this is only the beginning."

4

AS THE OTHER FAIRIES sat down to rest, Tink began to pace. She was sure she could come up with an idea that would work. She tugged at her bangs, thinking hard.

Down in the meadow near the dairy barn, the faint sound of bells could be heard. Cannonball or no cannonball, the dairy mice had to be fed. The mouse-herding-talent fairies were taking the herd out to pasture.

Tink looked toward the meadow. "Mice!" she said suddenly.

"Mice?" said two of the fairies nearest to her.

"Yes," said Tink. "Mice. It's simple. We'll harness all the dairy mice to the cannonball. Maybe, together, all of them can move it!"

"Wonderful idea, Tink!" said Queen Clarion.

The messenger-talent fairies headed for the pasture to tell the mouse-herding fairies to round up the dairy mice. Meanwhile, the kitchen-talent fairies hurried back to the kitchen to collect all the loaves of acorn bread they could spare. The mice adored acorn bread. Occasionally, a mouse would get loose from the herd and be caught in the Home Tree pantry, nibbling bread. Now the fairies could use the bread as a lure to get the mice to pull the ball.

Fairies from other talents pitched in too. Florian and the rest of the weaving-talent fairies quickly fashioned ropes from sweet grass they'd plucked from the meadow.

"I wish we had time to collect marsh grass," Florian said. "It makes a stronger rope. But I think this should do."

It only took a few minutes for the mouse-herders to get the mice to the Home Tree. One by one, the fairies began to harness the mice to the rope. Altogether, there were thirty-six mice. They stood at attention, their noses quivering.

At last, they were all in formation. The mouse-herding fairies stood just in front of them, waving the bread. The mice squeaked excitedly at the sight and smell of it.

"That's it, my little loves," said one of the mouse herders. "Delicious bread!

Come and get it."

She stepped back a little. The mice strained toward her. "Come on," the fairy urged. "Acorn bread! More than you've ever had before. You can have it all if you just try!"

And the mice did try. They loved that bread more than anything, much more than the sweetgrass seeds they were usually fed. They strained toward the bread. Their little claws dug into the ground. The courtyard echoed with the sounds of their squeaking.

The other fairies cheered them on. "You can do it, mice!" they yelled. "Get the bread! Move the ball! You can do it!"

The ball wobbled. The mice leaned into their harnesses – and the ball moved. Not a lot, maybe half an inch. But it moved.

"It's working, Tink!" cried Terence. He gave her an enormous smile and clapped her on the back.

"It's working! It's working!" other fairies echoed.

Tink's face was flushed. Her eyes shone. All her attention was focused on the cannonball. It moved another half inch, and –

Snap!

The rope around the cannonball broke. The mice leaped forward, suddenly free from the weight. They lunged at the bread in the mouse-herders' hands and quickly began to gobble it down.

The fairies stopped in mid-cheer. Everyone let out a disappointed sigh.

"Marsh grass," said Florian. She shook her head. "It always makes a stronger rope."

Tink flew over to look at the mice. They were still panting from the effort of pulling the ball. Their furry sides heaved in and out.

"Do you think they could do it again?" she asked one of the mouse-herding fairies. "If we made a stronger rope, that is."

The fairy shook her head. "I don't think so," she said. "It might wear them out. Dairy mice can be quite delicate, you know. If they get too tired, they stop giving milk."

Tink's shoulders slumped. But she tried hard not to show her disappointment. "Well," she said, "it was a good try. We'll just have to think of something else."

Queen Clarion spoke up. "Maybe that's enough work for one day," she said gently. "The cannonball won't go anywhere before tomorrow. Why don't we all get cleaned up and have some dinner?"

The fairies murmured their agreement. Not only were they all tired, they were also very hungry.

As the other fairies headed into the Home Tree, Tink lingered behind.

Well, Tink, you wanted a challenge, she said to herself. *And now you've got one.*

She stared up at the huge cannonball. *But am I up to it?* she wondered.

5

BECAUSE THE KITCHEN was such a mess, dinner that night was simple – acorn-butter sandwiches with dandelion salad. The tired fairies ate quickly. The sun had already set. After a long, hard day of work, they were eager to go to bed.

As soon as she was done eating, Tink realised she had a problem. She had nowhere to sleep. She watched as the other fairies headed for their rooms. In all the excitement over the cannonball, they had forgotten that Tink didn't have her own room to go to.

The tearoom slowly emptied. Tink remained sitting at her table. She wasn't sure what to do. As the shadows lengthened, she felt more and more forlorn.

At last Rani noticed Tink sitting alone. She realized the problem at once.

"Tink," she said, "what will you do tonight?"

"I think maybe I'll just sleep outside," Tink replied bravely. "I can use a maple leaf as a blanket."

"You can sleep in my room," Rani told her. "It's better than sleeping outside, anyway."

"Okay," Tink said. She felt relieved. "I would like that. I'm awfully tired."

Tink followed Rani up to her room. She had visited Rani's room many times before. But until that evening, she hadn't noticed the details. She looked around at the blue-green walls and the seaweed curtains hanging in the windows. The floor was paved with smooth river stones.

It seemed like a quiet, peaceful place. Tink was looking forward to a good night's sleep.

"Shall we play a game of seashell tiddlywinks?" Rani asked.

"Not tonight," said Tink. She really was exhausted. "I think I'm ready to go to bed. Where should I sleep?"

"I could pile lots of blankets on the floor," Rani suggested.

"Let me help you," said Tink.

Together they piled woven-fern blankets on the floor until they had made a soft bed.

"That should be very comfortable," Tink said when they were done. But she could not help noticing how humid Rani's room was. Even the blankets felt damp.

Tink settled herself on the pile. She was so tired, she was sure she'd fall asleep in a moment.

Rani covered her up with a sheet, which was also slightly damp. "Good night, dear friend," she said. Then she climbed into her own bed, which was made from driftwood. She pulled the seaweed quilt up to her chin.

Tink lay on her back, gazing at the blue-green ceiling. *It was nice of Rani to take me in*, she thought. Then she closed her eyes and gave in to her tiredness.

Seconds later, Tink opened her eyes. She could feel a lump beneath the pile of blankets. It was one of the river stones that paved the floor.

Tink tried turning on her side, but

that was no better. She flopped over on her stomach, but that was worse still. She ended up on her back again.

Tink thought wistfully of her comfy loaf-pan bed and the soft, dappled light that came through the colander lampshades in her room. How she loved to fall asleep beneath the still life of the stockpot, whisk, and griddle. And now it was gone, all gone. Tink sighed.

Moonlight filtered in through the seaweed curtains. Suddenly Tink gasped and jumped up. Two long arms seemed to reach out to her from the corner of the room.

Rani heard her and sat straight up. "What's the matter?" she cried.

"Th-there's something in the corner!"

whispered Tink. She was almost too scared to breathe.

"Where? I don't see it!" whispered Rani. She followed the direction of Tink's pointing finger. But the room was too dark. They couldn't see clearly.

Quickly, Rani lit her scallop-shell lamp. Then she started to giggle. "That's just my clothes hanging on a clothes tree, Tink. It's made from a coral branch. Remember?"

Gradually, Tink's heart stopped racing. Her breath returned to normal. "Oh," she said. "So it is." Now she felt foolish. She wished more than ever that she could be in her own bed.

Rani turned out the light. They settled back down to sleep.

Tink tried to drift off, she really did.

But the paving rocks were not getting any softer. And then she became aware of another thing.

Drip. Drip. Drip-drip. Drip.

Drip. Drip. Drip-drip. Drip.

It was a slow, steady rhythm. Tink had forgotten all about Rani's drip. She had a permanent leak in her room, whether it was raining or not. Beneath the leak sat a bucket made from a human-sized thimble. Inside the bucket, a Never minnow swam contentedly around and around.

Drip. Drip. Drip-drip. Drip.

By now, Tink had given up trying to sleep. She lay on her back and stared at the ceiling. Every now and then she shifted her wings under the damp sheet to find a better position.

Sometime before dawn, Tink heard a new noise. It was Rani crying.

"Rani," whispered Tink, "are you all right?"

There was no answer, just more crying. Tink brightened her glow so she could see Rani a little better. Rani was sound asleep, weeping onto her pillow. The air in the room was getting damper and damper.

"Rani," Tink tried again. "Wake up. You're having a bad dream."

Still Rani did not wake. Tink finally gave up and went back to staring at the ceiling. She listened to the dripping water and Rani's crying.

A little after dawn, Rani awoke. She sat up in bed and stretched her arms toward the ceiling. "I just had the most wonderful dream!" she said when she saw that Tink was awake.

"No, you didn't. You had an awful dream," Tink snapped. She was fairly cross, having not slept a wink the whole night.

Rani gave her a strange look and shook her head. "No, it was long and wonderful," she said. "I was playing with a big ball of water. I was tossing it back and forth with Silvermist and Tally. We could throw it as high as the top of the Home Tree and make a rainbow in the sunlight. It was so beautiful!"

Now it was Tink's turn to give Rani a strange look. "But you were crying," she insisted. "Cupfuls. Buckets. Barrels. Feel your bed, it's all – "

Rani broke into a big grin. " – wet," she finished. "I was crying in the dream, too! Crying from happiness!"

Tink just shook her head. She got up from her damp, lumpy bed. "Rani," she said, "you are my very good friend. But I am a pots-and-pans fairy and you are a water fairy, and I will never truly understand you." She smiled and gave Rani a hug.

Rani's eyes filled with tears again. "You're my good friend, too. And I'll never really understand you, either," she said, hugging Tink back. She wiped her eyes with a leafkerchief. "Do you want to go have some breakfast?"

"Yes," said Tink. "But my wings are too damp to fly."

Rani picked up another leafkerchief and gently dried Tink's wings. Then they went downstairs for breakfast.

6

BREAKFAST WAS VERY GOOD, as usual. Platters of Dulcie's wonderful pumpkin muffins and pots of blackberry tea sat on every table in the tearoom. But no breakfast would have been delicious enough to cheer Tink up that morning.

Tink was tired. She was damp. And she wanted her room back.

She stared gloomily at the serving platter in front of her. It reminded her of her platter–frying-pan–spoon chair.

"Rough night?" asked Angus. He was sitting next to Tink at the pots-and-pans-talent table.

"Just a little damp," said Tink with a sigh. She took a sip of tea. "But don't worry. I'm ready to get to work. I'll have that cannonball out of Pixie Hollow in no time." Even to her own ears, she did not sound very sure.

"Tinker Bell!" a cheerful voice exclaimed. Tink turned around. Gwinn, a tiny decoration-talent fairy, was beaming at her. "Are you ready to start putting your room back together?" Gwinn asked. "Cedar and I are heading up there now to get started." She gestured at Cedar, who was standing behind her.

Cedar was the biggest, strongest looking fairy Tinker Bell had ever seen. She was nearly six inches tall! It was clear from the hammer and saw Cedar was carrying that she was a carpenter-talent fairy.

Cedar nodded shyly in greeting.

Her great height made Gwinn look even tinier.

"Usually, we prepare rooms for fairies who have just arrived in Never Land," Gwinn continued. She spoke very, very fast. Tink had to concentrate to keep up. "Of course, we don't know them yet. So we just make our best guess about what that fairy might want. And then we hope she likes it. But you're already *here!* I've never helped a fairy decorate her own room before! You can tell me exactly what you want! It will be perfect! *Perfect!* Right, Cedar?"

Cedar nodded and stared bashfully at the ground.

Tink bit her lip. She wanted to start rebuilding her room. But she had promised to get rid of the cannonball.

Angus read her mind. "You can work on the cannonball later, Tink, after you and Gwinn decide what your new room should look like," he pointed out.

Tink thought about it for a moment. Angus was right. The cannonball could wait.

"All right," Tink said. She smiled. "Let's go!"

A short time later, Tink was watching Cedar hammer planks into the walls of her new room.

Gwinn flew from one corner to the next, measuring the space with her eyes. She kept up a steady stream of chatter.

"You'll want silver paint," Gwinn told Tink. "Or maybe gold. Or something copper? Ooh, yes! Copper could be just lovely with the sunlight coming in – "

"Silver will be fine," said Tink, trying to keep up.

"And I suppose you'd like colander lampshades again," Gwinn went on. "Although a nice iris-petal lantern would give the room a softer look… "

"Colanders, please," Tink cut in. She was surprised to find she was having fun.

"And you'll need curtains, a bedspread, some kind of rug… " Gwinn zipped from corner to corner. She was making Tink dizzy.

Tink sat down in the middle of the bare floor to watch her.

Gwinn will make sure that the walls are the right color, Tink thought. *And she will get new colanders for the lamps.* But Gwinn couldn't make her another stilllife painting. And Cedar couldn't make her another loaf-pan bed.

If I want my room back just the way it was, Tink thought, *I'm going to have to take matters into my own hands.*

"I'll be back in a little while," she told Gwinn and Cedar.

Cedar mumbled good-bye through a mouthful of nails. Gwinn absent-mindedly waved some curtain fabric at her. Tink flew out through the open ceiling and over the woods of Pixie Hollow.

Soon, Tink arrived at Bess's studio. It was made from an old tangerine crate that the art-talent fairy had set up in a remote clearing in the woods, where she could paint in peace and quiet.

Tink found Bess hard at work. She was painting a portrait of an animal-talent fairy. The animal-talent fairy posed on a cushion, holding her favorite ladybird on her lap.

"Tink!" Bess said. She set down her brush and hugged her friend. "What a terrible thing to happen to your room. Is there anything I can do to help?"

"Actually, there is," said Tink. She explained that she needed another still life of a stockpot, whisk, and griddle to hang over her bed.

Bess looked a little embarrassed. "Oh, Tink," she said unhappily. "Of *course* I'll paint a new picture for you. But I won't be able to get to it for a while. I've already promised paintings to five other fairies."

The animal-talent fairy cleared her throat impatiently. The ladybug on her lap was getting restless. Bess gave Tink another hug, and then got back to work.

Tink flew off, trying not to feel discouraged. Her next stop was the kitchen. She hoped to find some pots and pans that were beyond repair. With luck, she could make another frying-pan chair exactly like her old one.

Dulcie met Tink at the kitchen door. She was carrying a tray of pretty little tea cakes. As Dulcie set the cakes on a windowsill to cool, Tink asked her if she had any pots, pans, spoons, whisks, or other kitchen items that she needed to get rid of.

"Well," replied Dulcie, "there was that salad fork with the bent tines. I was ready to give up on it. But Angus fixed it last week. It's been perfectly pointy and prongy ever since."

The other pots-and-pans fairies are too good at their jobs, Tink thought. She tugged at her bangs and gave a frustrated sigh. She didn't want to make a chair out of objects that were still useful.

Tink could usually fix almost anything. But here was something that couldn't be fixed, at least not right away.

"Grrr!" cried Tink. She shot three inches into the air with sheer frustration. Her room was smashed, and even when it was fixed, it still wouldn't feel like her room. After all, *where* was she going to find another loaf-pan bed?

That cannonball will regret the day it fell into Pixie Hollow, Tink vowed. *And Captain Hook will regret it even more.*

7

TINK ZOOMED into the courtyard. She flew right up to the cannonball and gave it a mighty kick.

Ow! Tink danced through the air, clutching her toes and grimacing in pain. A few fairies who had been flying by stared at Tink in astonishment.

Once her toes stopped hurting, Tink found that she felt much calmer. But now she was more determined than ever to get rid of the big, bad ball.

"This cannonball is going to move!" she cried. "I am going to banish it from Pixie Hollow once and for all. But I'm going to need help from every fairy and sparrow man. Together, we can do it! Now, who's with me?"

But the other fairies didn't jump up as Tink hoped they would.

"I don't know. Maybe we could learn to live with the cannonball," said one of the decoration-talent fairies. "We could probably fix it up to make it look nice."

The other decoration-talent fairies brightened a bit. "We could!" one agreed. "We could decorate it with hollyhock garlands and daisy chains."

"Or we could paint it a pretty shade of green to sort of blend in," said another. "Maybe a nice sage color."

"But... but don't you want to get rid of it?" Tink asked, astonished.

"Well, of course we do, Tink," said Beck, who happened to be in the courtyard. "But we want to get back to doing what we usually do. We're all busy with our own talents."

Tink couldn't believe what she was hearing. Were the other fairies giving up already, before they'd even tried?

"We have fun in the courtyard, don't we?" she said. "It's part of our home. How will we feel looking at this cannonball every time we come out of the Home Tree? We'll never be able to have a meeting or a party here again. Even if it's decorated and painted, it will still take up too much room."

Several fairies murmured in agreement. But no one volunteered to help.

"We tried moving it yesterday, and we couldn't," a water-talent sparrow man pointed out.

"I know we can do this," Tink

replied. "We just have to figure out how."

Just then, Terence flew up. He was holding a teacup in one hand. In his other hand was a sack of fairy dust.

"Tink, you didn't get your fairy dust yet today, did you?" he said.

As a dust-talent sparrow man, Terence handed out dust to all the fairies and sparrow men in Pixie Hollow. Every-one got one teacupful per day. The dust was what allowed the fairies to fly and do magic.

As Terence poured the magical dust over Tink, her eyes widened. "That's it! I know how we can move the cannonball!" she cried.

The fairies in the courtyard perked up. "How, Tink?" Terence asked.

"We move big things with balloon

carriers, right?" Tink said. Balloon carriers were baskets attached to fairy-dust-filled balloons. The fairies used them to move things that were too heavy to carry. "That's what we'll do with the cannonball. We'll build a giant balloon and use lots of extra fairy dust to give it more lift. We can float the cannonball away."

"It's a good idea," said Terence. The other fairies nodded. Even Angus looked impressed.

"Send word to the other dust-talent fairies," Tink told Terence. "We'll need all the fairy dust they can spare. The rest of us will get the balloon carrier ready."

This was easier said than done. In order to attach the balloon to the cannonball, they would need heavy ropes. Tink found Florian and explained her plan.

"We'll use marsh grass this time," Florian said with certainty. "And we'll make it extra thick."

She got the weaving-talent fairies together, and they set out to collect long strands of tough marsh grasses, which they would weave into the strongest ropes they could make.

Next, Tink went to the sewing-talent fairies. She asked them to make a silk balloon, the biggest one Pixie Hollow had ever seen.

Some of the fairies grumbled. They didn't want to leave the pretty petal dresses and leaf-frock coats they were working on. But Tink's spirit was catching.

Soon, they were collecting every spare scrap of spider silk to make the giant balloon.

It was afternoon by the time the weaving-talent fairies finished making the ropes. But they looked sturdy this time. They were nearly as thick as a fairy's waist.

The weavers secured the ropes around the bottom of the cannonball. Then it was time to attach the balloon. The sewing-talent fairies sewed the ends of each rope to the edges of the balloon.

Tink oversaw all this work. She paced back and forth, worrying. Would the balloon lift off? Would the cannonball stay attached? What if this idea didn't work either?

At last, the whole contraption was

ready to go. It was time for the dust-talent fairies and sparrow men to do their work.

By now a crowd had gathered. Everyone watched, hardly daring to breathe, as Terence and a dust-talent sparrow man named Jerome began to fill the balloon with fairy dust. Instead of the teacups they usually used to hand out the dust, they scooped up great mounds of it with shovels they had borrowed from the garden-talent fairies.

The balloon started to rise – up, up, up. The fairies watched in wonder. Soon the balloon was completely inflated. It strained against the ropes.

The ropes pulled taut, but the cannonball stayed stubbornly on the ground.

"More fairy dust!" cried Tink.

Terence and Jerome flew up to the top of the balloon and sprinkled more shovelfuls of dust onto it. They sprinkled some dust onto the cannonball for good measure. The balloon strained harder and harder. All the fairies and sparrow men strained with it. Their muscles were tense. Their wings vibrated in sheer concentration. The fairies glowed brightly as they willed the balloon to rise.

And finally, it did! The grass ropes pulled tauter, and the cannonball could resist no longer. It lifted off the ground.

"It's going!" shouted Tink.

First it rose just a hair off the ground, no more than the thickness of a fairy's wing. Then it reached the height of two hairs. Then it was almost as high up as a fairy's knee, and then higher than a fairy's head. It was working! It was really working!

If the fairies and sparrow men had not been so caught up in the progress of the cannonball, they might have noticed that a strong breeze had sprung up. But they did not notice, until –

Pow!

Hisssssss.

"What was that?" Tink cried in alarm.

What it was, they soon discovered, was a horse chestnut. The spiky green globe had fallen from a nearby horse chestnut tree. And the wind had been blowing in just the right direction to push it into the balloon. The horse chestnut's spikes had pierced the delicate spider silk.

The hissing lasted only a second. The cannonball landed back in the courtyard with a great thud. Inside the tree, delicate cups and saucers could be heard shattering in the tearoom.

The fairies groaned.

"Well, that's the end of that," Angus said.

But that wasn't the end. For the cannonball had gotten just the start it needed. It began to roll.

8

"THE BALL!" Rani cried. "L-look out!"

Several fairies leaped out of the way in the nick of time. There was a very slight slope away from the Home Tree, but that was enough. The cannonball rolled down it.

"Hooray!" a decoration-talent fairy yelled. "Good-bye, ball!"

"Good riddance!" added a butterfly herder. Other fairies joined in the cheering.

But Tink followed the ball's progress, frowning.

"It's great that we got it going, but – " she began.

"Now we don't know *where* it's going," Rani finished for her.

"Exactly," said Tink.

The ball began to pick up speed. The fairies' cheers died out.

"It was so hard to start," Terence said worriedly. "But now it's going to be impossible to stop!"

"Maybe it will just roll into a tree or something," said Beck.

"If we're lucky," said Angus.

"I think we'd better follow it!" cried Tink. And the fairies leaped into the air to chase after the ball.

The cannonball was rolling fast now. It bounced across a tree root and rolled over a hillock of grass. It was headed for Havendish Stream.

"It's going to hit the mill!" cried Jerome.

This was truly a disaster. The mill

was one of the most important places in Pixie Hollow. The tree-picking-talent fairies ground grains and nuts into baking flour there. And the dust-talent fairies used the mill to grind Mother Dove's feathers into fairy dust. It was also where the fairy dust was stored – all of it. An entire year's supply.

At once, the same picture flashed through every fairy and sparrow man's mind: the mill smashed, the fairy dust inside blowing away with the wind. They would be unable to fly, unable to do magic. How would they even build another mill if they did not have the power of fairy dust?

A startled rabbit poked his head out of his burrow. But when he saw the cannonball rolling toward him, he quickly dove back inside.

The cannonball rolled over a large toadstool, flattening it. The fairies flew helplessly behind. They could hardly bring themselves to watch.

But just before it reached the mill, the cannonball hit a good-sized rock. It jumped into the air and changed course. Instead of crashing into the mill, the ball splashed into the stream just above it. And there it stopped, wedged against the bank.

The fairies breathed sighs of relief all around. They laughed and hugged each other with joy. The mill was saved!

But Tink was not laughing. She did not take her eyes from the ball. As she watched, the water of Havendish Stream began to back up around it.

"Oh, no!" she said. "The stream is blocked!"

Everyone stared in disbelief. Tink was right. The ball had landed in the narrow branch of the stream that fed the mill. The water slowed to a trickle.

A few minnows had been thrown from the stream by the force of the cannonball's splash. They lay flopping on the bank. With cries of alarm, the animal-talent fairies raced to help them. They scooped the little fish up in their hands and dropped them back in the water.

This was not good. Not good at all. If the stream stopped running, the mill wheel would stop turning.

Indeed, they all heard the mill grind to a stop.

Rani started to cry, and it was not from happiness.

Why didn't I think of this? Tink asked herself angrily. *Why didn't it occur to me that once the ball started rolling, it was anybody's guess where it would end up?*

She sank down to the ground. She felt completely defeated. She had taken on a challenge that was too big. And she had failed. What was going to happen to Pixie Hollow now?

"Well, Tink," someone said. Tink looked up. Queen Clarion was standing next to her. "I guess it's time for you to come up with another idea," the queen said seriously.

This took Tink by surprise. She had thought the story was over. The ball was stuck in the stream. There was certainly no way to move it now.

But Rani was nodding and smiling through her tears. "We know you can figure this out, Tink," she said. "Look how many things you've already thought of. There has to be one more thing."

Tink was astounded. Not only did the others have hope that the problem could be solved, they thought she could solve it.

Rani is right, she thought. *There has to be one more thing.* Tink knew she had a responsibility to figure out what that one thing was. The other fairies were counting on her.

"Yes, Tink," said Florian. "It's time for your next idea. Do you want us to leave you alone?"

"Or would you like some nice

soup while you think?" said one of the cooking-talent fairies, who specialised in cucumber soup.

"No soup," Tink said, squaring her shoulders. "I'm just going to think."

9

TINK FLITTED around the whole terrible scene, trying to focus. It was hard looking at the mess the cannonball had made. Water was starting to flood the banks of the stream, turning them into muddy pools. Toadstools and wildflowers had been squashed and flattened when the ball rolled over them. The cannonball had also plowed through a pile of acorns that the tree-picking-talent fairies had set aside to be ground in the mill. Now little chips of acorn littered the landscape.

Tink stared at them. They reminded her of something.

Little chips of acorn, she thought. *Little chips...*

"I've got it!" she hollered. "I've got

the solution! I was thinking about it the wrong way the whole time! The cannonball is a huge thing, right?" said Tink. "It was much too heavy for us to move. And we certainly couldn't control it once it started moving. But even if we can't move a huge thing, we can move lots of *little* things."

Queen Ree nodded her head in understanding. "Of course!" she said.

"Of course *what?*" said a few fairies who hadn't caught on.

"We're going to break the cannonball into lots of tiny pieces and move them out of Pixie Hollow," Tink declared.

"Spring!" She turned to the message-talent fairy. "Ask the other pots-and-pans fairies to bring all the hammers and chisels they have in their workshops. And the carpenter-talent fairies – they have hammers and chisels, too!"

"I have a couple of chisels," said an art-talent fairy. "For making sculptures."

"Great!" said Tink. "Let's round up all the tools we have. We're going to break this cannonball up!"

A short time later, an array of tools was laid out on the grass next to the cannon-ball. The sand-sorting-talent fairies had piled sandbags around the ball, to hold back the stream. That way, the fairies wouldn't get wet as they worked.

Tink grabbed a hammer and chisel and flew to the top of the cannonball. As the best pots-and-pans fairy in Pixie Hollow, Tink knew a lot about metal. For example, she knew that every piece of metal had a weak point.

She put her ear close to the cannonball. Then she began to tap it with her hammer, inching across the surface.

Bing, bing, bing, bing, bing, bing, bing, bing, bing, bing, bong, bing…

Tink stopped. She went back and tapped the spot again.

Bong!

Tink had found the cannonball's weak spot. Holding the tip of her chisel against the ball, Tink whacked it with the hammer as hard as she could. A crack appeared.

Tink whacked it again. The crack grew.

"Everybody take a hammer and chisel!" Tink told the other fairies.

"Even if your talent is completely unrelated to breaking up cannonballs, give it a try. You might like it."

The fairies got to work. As they wedged their chisels into the iron, more cracks appeared. The air started to ring with the sound of metal banging into metal. It was a sound Tink loved with all her heart.

"I like this!" said one of the cooking-talent fairies, whose specialty was making ice sculptures. "It's just like chipping ice. But you don't have to be careful!"

Gradually, the cracks in the cannonball grew. Pieces began to break off. The fairies laid them on the bank of Havendish Stream.

Soon they had broken the whole cannonball apart. A mound of

iron bits sat by the stream.

"What are we going to do with all this?" said Twire, a scrap-metal-recovery-talent fairy. "It's more iron than we could use in an entire year in Pixie Hollow."

Tink nodded. But she wasn't really focused on what Twire was saying. She was getting another idea.

Quietly, she waved Terence over. "I want to ask your opinion about something," she said. "About fairy-dust magic." She whispered her idea into Terence's ear.

Terence scratched his head thoughtfully.

"I think it can be done," he said finally. "It will take a great deal of fairy dust. And the magic won't be easy. We'll have to concentrate.

But I think it could work."

"That's what I hoped," said Tink.

She flew back to where the other fairies were still working. They were almost finished breaking apart the cannonball.

Tink stood on one of the bigger pieces of iron to make her announcement.

"Fairies," she said, "we're going to get this cannonball out of Pixie Hollow once and for all."

The fairies cheered.

"But what are we going to do with it?" asked Rani.

Tink smiled and said with a wink, "We're going to give it back to Captain Hook, of course."

10

SHOUTING WITH GLEE, the fairies gathered up the pieces of cannonball. There were many more pieces than there were fairies. So each fairy took as many as she could fly with. Gwinn took one big piece. Cedar took six small ones. Tink herself carried three pieces, and it took all her strength to lift off.

Meanwhile, Jerome and Terence were inside the mill filling sacks full of fairy dust, as much as they could carry.

When everything was ready, the fairies lifted into the air. It was quite a sight, for those who could see it: a great cloud of fairies flying over the lush landscape of Never Land, headed for Pirate Cove. Of course, the pirates themselves could not see the fairies, who were invisible to them. If Captain Hook had looked up just then, he would have seen hundreds of chips of iron miraculously bobbing through the air.

But Captain Hook was not looking up. As the fairies approached the cove, they could see the vile-tempered pirate rowing a small boat through the water near the shore. He was muttering to himself.

"I'll teach that ridiculous boy a lesson," he growled. "Throw my best cutlass into the sea, will he? Thinks he can get the best of me, does he? Well, we'll see about that, Master Peter Pan. Let's see how you like a cannonball for your dinner tonight."

As Hook rowed, he looked down through the shallow water. Evidently, he was trying to find his lost cutlass.

The fairies were right above Hook's little rowboat. They hovered there, still in a cloud. "Okay!" Tink cried. "Start bringing the pieces together!"

The fairies flew nearer to each other. They began to fit the pieces of cannonball together.

"Now the fairy dust!" Tink commanded.

Terence and the other dust-talent fairies and sparrow men began to throw handfuls of fairy dust over the ball. Magically, the iron chips snapped into place like pieces of a jigsaw puzzle. The fairies concentrated, using all the magic they could muster.

In moments, the cannonball was complete. It was just as it had been when it crashed into Pixie Hollow.

And, of course, once it was whole, it was too heavy for the fairies to hold any longer. It fell from their grasp and plummeted toward Captain Hook's rowboat.

Hook looked up just in time to see a cannonball fall from thin air.

"What – " was all he had time to say before the ball crashed into the floor of his rowboat. It broke through the wood and fell to the bottom of the sea.

At once, the boat filled with water. Hook had no choice but to abandon ship. He swam to shore as the rowboat slowly sank.

The sun was setting as the fairies flew back to Pixie Hollow, glad to finally be rid of the cannonball.

The next day, Pixie Hollow had just about returned to normal. Havendish Stream flowed between its banks, which looked none the worse for wear. The mill was turning once again. And fairies from several different talents had pitched in to help repair the courtyard.

The cooking-talent fairies had spent the day making acorn soup, muffins, cookies, and bread with the acorns that had been smashed by the cannonball. Everyone was good and sick of acorns. But all the broken ones had been just about used up, and nothing had gone to waste.

After her wet night in Rani's room, Tink had decided to sleep outside until her room was rebuilt. She'd found a nook between two branches where she would be sheltered from the wind and safe from owls. She had actually been quite happy out there, looking at the stars through the leaves of the Home Tree.

And in the morning, what had she found by the roots of a nearby tree but her loaf-pan bed! It had one big dent in it. *Challenging to fix*, Tink thought. *But not too challenging.*

Later that day, Gwinn and Cedar helped Tink carry the bed up to her new room. They had worked all night to get it ready for her.

When Gwinn opened the door, Tink was speechless with delight. Her new room had colander lamps just like the old ones. The walls were painted with silver paint to make them look as if they were made of tin. And best of all, Bess had manged to finish a new painting for Tink after all. It was another still life of a stockpot, whisk, and griddle – and it was twice the size of the old one.

"It's beautiful," she managed to say at last.

Gwinn and Cedar helped Tink put her bed back into place. Then Gwinn took another look around the room. "You know," she said thoughtfully, "we could decorate with tiny cannonballs, Tink. So you'd always remember your greatest. challenge."

"It's an interesting thought," said Tink. "But I'm all through with cannonballs."

Just then, Dulcie came hurrying up to Tink's room. She poked her head in the open door and waved a metal sheet.

"Tink," she said, "do you think you could fix this baking sheet for me? I have one last batch of acorn cookies to put in the oven. It just has a little hole. I know it's hardly worth your attention. Not much of a challenge."

"Believe me," said Tink, "that is just fine with me."

And taking the sheet from Dulcie's hands, she headed for her workshop, whistling.

The
Trouble
with
Tink

1

ONE SUNNY, BREEZY afternoon in Pixie Hollow, Tinker Bell sat in her workshop, frowning at a copper pot. With one hand, she clutched her tinker's hammer, and with the other, she tugged at her blond fringe, which was Tink's habit when she was thinking hard about something. The pot had been squashed nearly flat on one side. Tink was trying to determine how to tap it to make it right again.

All around Tink lay her tinkering tools: baskets full of rivets, scraps of tin, pliers, iron wire, and swatches of steel wool for scouring a pot until it shone. On the walls hung portraits of some of the pans and ladles and washtubs Tink had mended. Tough jobs were always Tink's favourites.

Tink was a pots-and-pans fairy, and her greatest joy came from fixing things. She loved anything metal that could be cracked or dented. Even her workshop was made from a teakettle that had once belonged to a Clumsy.

Ping! Ping! Ping! Tink began to pound away. Beneath Tink's hammer the copper moved as easily as if she were smoothing the folds in a blanket.

Tink had almost finished when a shadow fell across her worktable. She looked up and saw a dark figure silhouetted in the sunny doorway. The edges of the silhouette sparkled.

"Oh, hi, Terence. Come in," said Tink.

Terence moved out of the sunlight and into the room, but he continued to shimmer. Terence was a dust-talent sparrow man. He measured and handed out the fairy dust that allowed Never Land's fairies to fly and do their magic. As a result, he was dustier than most fairies, and he sparkled all the time.

"Hi, Tink. Are you working? I mean, I see you're working. Are you almost done? That's a nice pot," Terence said, all in a rush.

"It's Violet's pot. They're dyeing spider silk tomorrow, and she needs it for boiling the dye," Tink replied. She looked eagerly at Terence's hands and sighed when she saw that they were empty. Terence stopped by Tink's workshop nearly every day. Often he brought a broken pan or a mangled sieve for her to fix. Other times, like now, he just brought himself.

"That's right, tomorrow is dyeing day," said Terence. "I saw the harvest talents bringing in the blueberries for the dye earlier. They've got a good crop this year, they should get a nice deep blue colour..."

As Terence rambled on, Tink looked longingly at the copper pot. She picked up her hammer, then reluctantly put it back down. *It would be rude to start tapping right now*, she thought. Tink liked talking to Terence. But she liked tinkering more.

"Anyway, Tink, I just wanted to let you know that they're starting a game of tag in the meadow. I thought maybe you'd like to join in," Terence finished.

Tink's wing tips quivered. It had been ages since there had been a game of fairy tag. Suddenly, she felt herself bursting with the desire to play, the way you fill up with a sneeze just before it explodes.

She glanced down at the pot again.

The dent was nearly smooth. Tink thought she could easily play a game of tag and still have time to finish her work before dinner.

Standing up, she slipped her tinker's hammer into a loop on her belt and smiled at Terence.

"Let's go," she said.

When Tink and Terence got to the meadow, the game of tag was already in full swing. Everywhere spots of bright colour wove in and out of the tall grass as fairies darted after each other.

Fairy tag is different from the sort of tag that humans, or Clumsies, as the fairies call them, play. For one thing, the fairies fly rather than run. For another, the fairies don't just chase each other until one is tagged "it." If that were the case, the fast-flying-talent fairies would win every time.

In fairy tag, the fairies and sparrow men all use their talents to try to win. And when a fairy is tagged, by being tapped on her head and told "Choose you," that fairy's whole talent group – or at least all those who are playing – becomes "chosen." Games of fairy tag are large, complicated, and very exciting.

As Tink and Terence joined the game, a huge drop of water came hurtling through the air at them. Terence ducked, and the drop splashed against a dandelion behind him. The water-talent fairies were "chosen," Tink realised.

As they sped through the tall grass, the water fairies hurled balls of water at the other fairies. When the balls hit, they burst like water balloons and dampened the fairies' wings. This slowed them down, which helped the water fairies gain on them.

Already the other talents had organised their defence. The animal-talent fairies, led by Beck and Fawn, had rounded up a crew of chipmunks to ride when their wings got too wet to fly. The light-talent fairies bent the sunshine as they flew through it, so rays of light always shone in the eyes of the fairies chasing them. Tink saw that the pots-and-pans fairies had used washtubs to create makeshift catapults. They were trying to catch the balls of water and fling them back at the water fairies.

As Tink zipped down to join them, she heard a voice above her call, "Watch out, Tinker Bell! I'll choose you!" She looked up. Her friend Rani, a water-talent fairy, was circling above her on the back of a dove. Rani was the only fairy in the kingdom who didn't have wings. She'd cut hers off to help save Never Land when Mother Dove's egg had been destroyed. Now Brother Dove did her flying for her.

Rani lifted her arm and hurled a water ball. It wobbled through the air and splashed harmlessly on the ground, inches away from Tink. Tink laughed, and so did Rani.

"I'm such a terrible shot!" Rani cried happily.

Just then, the pots-and-pans fairies fired a catapult. The water flew at Rani and drenched her. Rani laughed even harder.

"Choose you!"

The shout rang through the meadow. All the fairies stopped midflight and turned. A water-talent fairy named Tally was standing over Jerome, a dust-talent sparrow man. Her hand was on his head.

"Dust talent!" Jerome sang out.

Abruptly, the fairies rearranged themselves. Anyone who happened to be near a dust-talent fairy immediately darted away. The other fairies hovered in the air, waiting to see what the dust talents would do.

Tink caught sight of Terence near a tree stump a few feet away. Terence grinned at her. She coyly smiled back – and then she bolted. In a flash, Terence was after her.

Tink dove into an azalea bush. Terence was right on her heels. Tink's sides ached with laughter, but she kept flying. She wove in and out of the bush's branches. She made a hairpin turn around a thick branch. Then she dashed toward an opening in the leaves and headed back to the open meadow.

But suddenly, the twigs in front of her closed like a gate. Tink skidded to a stop and watched as the twigs wrapped around themselves. With a flick of fairy dust, Terence had closed the branches of the bush. It was the simplest magic. But Tink was trapped.

She turned as Terence flew up to her.

"Choose you," he said, placing his hand on her head. But he said it softly. None of the rest of the fairies could have heard.

Just then, a shout rang out across the meadow: "Hawk!"

At once, Tink and Terence dropped down under the azalea bush's branches. Through the leaves, Tink could see the other fairies ducking for cover. The scout who had spotted the hawk hid in the branches of a nearby elm tree. The entire meadow seemed to hold its breath as the hawk's shadow moved across it.

When it was gone, the fairies waited a few moments, then slowly came out of their hiding places. But the mood had changed. The game of tag was over.

Tink and Terence climbed out of the bush.

"I must finish Violet's pot before dinner," Tink told Terence. "Thank you for telling me about the game."

"I'm really glad you came, Tink," said Terence. He gave her a sparkling smile, but Tink didn't see it. She was already flying away, thinking about the copper pot.

Tink's fingers itched to begin working

again. As she neared her workshop, she reached for her tinker's hammer hanging on her belt. Her fingertips touched the leather loop.

Tink stopped flying. Frantically, she ran her fingers over the belt loop again and again. Her hammer was gone.

2

TINK SKIMMED OVER the ground, back the way she'd come. Her eyes darted this way and that. She was hoping to catch a glimmer of metal in the tall grass.

"Fool," Tink told herself. "You foolish, foolish fairy."

When she reached the meadow, her heart sank. The trees on the far side of the meadow cast long shadows across the ground. To Tink, the meadow looked huge, like a vast jungle of waving grass and wildflowers. How would she ever find her hammer in there?

Just then, her eyes fell on the azalea bush. *Of course!* Tink thought. *I must have dropped it when I was dodging Terence.*

Tink flew to the bush. She checked the

ground beneath it and checked each branch. She paid particular attention to the places where a pots-and-pans fairy's hammer might get caught. Then she checked them again. And again. But the hammer was nowhere in sight.

Fighting back tears, Tink flew across the open meadow. She tried to recall her zigzagging path in the tag game. Eventually she gave that up and began to search the meadow inch by inch, flying close to the ground. She parted the petals of wild-flowers. She peered into rabbit burrows. She looked everywhere she could think of, even places she knew the hammer couldn't possibly be.

As Tink searched, the sun sank into a red pool on the horizon, then disappeared. A thin sliver of moon rose in the sky. The night was so dark that even if Tink had flown over the hammer, she wouldn't have been able to see it. But the hammer was already long gone. A Never crow had spotted it hours before and, attracted by its shine, had carried it off to its nest.

The grass was heavy with dew by the time Tink slowly started back to the Home Tree. As she flew, tears of frustration rolled down her cheeks. She swiped them away. *What will I do without my hammer?* Tink wondered. It was her most important tool. She thought of the copper pot waiting patiently for her in her workshop, and more tears sprang to her eyes.

It might seem that it should have been easy for Tink to get another tinker's hammer, but in fact, it was not. In the fairy kingdom, there is just the right amount of everything; no more, no less. A tool-making fairy would need Never iron to make a new hammer. And a mining-talent fairy would have to collect the iron. Because their work was difficult, the mining-talent fairies only mined once in a moon cycle, when the moon was full. Tink eyed the thin silver slice in the sky. Judging from the moon, that wouldn't be for many days.

For a pots-and-pans fairy, going many days without fixing pots or pans would be like not eating or sleeping. To Tink, the idea was horrible.

But that wasn't the only reason she was crying. Tink had a secret. She *did* have a spare hammer. But it was at Peter Pan's hideout – she had accidentally left it there quite a while before. And she was terribly scared about going back to get it.

Tink got back to the Home Tree, but she was too upset to go inside and sleep. Instead, she flew up to the highest branch and perched there. She looked up at the stars and tried to figure out what to do.

Tink thought about Peter Pan: his wild red hair, his freckled nose turned up just so, his eyes that looked so happy when he laughed. She remembered the time that she and Peter had gone to the beach to skip rocks on the lagoon. One of the rocks had accidentally nicked a mermaid's tail as she dove beneath the water. The mermaid had scolded them so ferociously that Peter and Tink had fled laughing all the way to the other side of the island.

Tink's heart ached. Remembering Peter Pan was something she almost never let herself do. Since he had brought the

Wendy to Never Land, Tink and Peter had hardly spoken.

No, Tink decided. She couldn't go to Peter's for the spare hammer. It would make her too sad.

"I'll make do without it," she told herself. What was a hammer, after all, but just another tool?

3

TINK SLEPT FITFULLY that night and woke before the other fairies. As the sky began to get lighter, she crept out of the Home Tree and flew down to the beach.

In one corner of the lagoon, there was a small cave that could only be entered at low tide. Tink flew in and landed on the damp ground. The floor of the cave was covered with sea-polished pebbles. This was where Peter had come to get stones for skipping on the water, Tink remembered.

Tink carefully picked her way through the rocks. Many of them were as big as her head. They were all smooth and shiny with seawater.

At last Tink picked up a reddish pebble the size and shape of a sunflower seed. She hefted it once into the air and caught it again.

"This might work," Tink said aloud into the empty cave.

Might work, her voice echoed back to her.

As the tide rose and the waves began to roll in, Tink flew out of the cave, gripping the pebble in her fist.

Back in her workshop, Tink used iron wire to bind the flat side of the rock to a twig. With a pinch of fairy dust, she tightened the wires so the rock was snug against the wood. She held up her makeshift hammer and looked at it.

"It's not so bad," she said. She tried to sound positive.

Taking a deep breath, Tink began to tap the copper pot.

Clank! Clank! Clank! Tink winced as the horrible sound echoed through her workshop. With each blow, the copper pot seemed to shudder.

"I'm sorry, I'm sorry!" Tink whispered to the pot. She tried to tap more gently.

The work took forever. Each strike with the pebble hammer left a tiny dent. Slowly, the bent copper straightened out. But the pot's smooth, shiny surface was now as pitted and pockmarked as the skin of a grapefruit.

Tink fought back tears. *It's no good*, she thought. *This pebble doesn't work at all!*

Tink raised her arm to give the pot one last tap. Just then, the pebble flew off the stick and landed with a clatter in a pile of tin scrap, as if to say it agreed.

Suddenly, the door of Tink's workshop burst open and a fairy flew in. She wore a gauzy dress tie-dyed in a fancy pattern of blues and greens. Her cheeks were bright splotches of pink. Corkscrews of curly red hair stood out in all directions from her head, and her hands were stained purple with berry juice. She looked as if she had been painted using all the colours in a watercolour box. It was Violet, the pot's owner, a dyeing-talent fairy.

"Tink! Thank goodness you're almost done with the... Oh!" Violet exclaimed. She stopped and stared. Tink was standing over the copper pot, gripping a twig as if she planned to beat it like a drum.

"Oh, Violet, hi. Yes, I'm, er... I'm done with the pot. That is, mostly," Tink said. She put down the twig. With the other hand, she tugged nervously at her fringe.

"It looks... uh... " Violet's voice trailed off as she eyed the battered pot. Tink was the best pots-and-pans fairy in the kingdom. Violet didn't want to sound as if she was criticising her work.

"It needs a couple of touch-ups, but I fixed the squashed part," Tink reassured her. "It's perfectly good for boiling dye in. We can try it now if you like."

The door of Tink's workshop opened again. Terence came in, carrying a ladle that was so twisted it looked as if it had been tied in a knot.

"Hi, Tink! I brought you a ladle to fix!" he called out. "Oh, hello, Violet! Dropping off?" he asked as he spied the copper pot.

"No... er, picking up," Violet said worriedly.

"Oh," said Terence. He looked back at the pot in surprise.

Tink filled a bucket with water from a rain barrel outside her workshop and brought it over to her worktable. As Violet and Terence watched, she poured the water into the copper pot.

"See?" Tink said to Violet. "It's good as – "

Just then, they heard a metallic creaking sound. Suddenly – *plink, plink, plink, plink!* One by one, tiny streams of water burst through the damaged copper. The pot looked more like a watering can than something to boil dye in.

"Oh!" Violet and Terence gasped. They turned to Tink, their eyes wide.

Tink felt herself blush, but she couldn't tear her eyes away from the leaking pot. She had never failed to fix a pot before, much less made it worse than it was when she got it.

The thing was, no fairy ever failed at her talent. To do so would mean you weren't really talented at all.

4

AFTER A LONG, awkward silence, Violet closed her mouth, cleared her throat, and said, "I can probably share a dye pot with someone else. I'll come back and get this later." With a last confused glance at Tink, she hurried out the door.

Terence was also confused, but he was in no hurry to leave. He set the twisted ladle down on Tink's workbench.

"Tink, you look tired," he said gently.

"I'm not tired," said Tink.

"Maybe you need to take a break," Terence suggested. But he wasn't at all sure what Tink needed. "Why don't we fly to the tearoom? On my way here, I smelled pumpkin muffins baking in the kitchen. They smelled deli – "

"I'm not hungry," Tink interrupted, although she was starving. She hadn't had breakfast, or dinner the night before. But the talents always sat together in the tearoom. Tink didn't feel like sitting at a table with the other pots-and-pans fairies right now.

Suddenly, Tink was irritated with Terence. If he hadn't told her about the tag game, she never would have lost her hammer. Tink knew she wasn't being fair. But she was upset and embarrassed, and she wanted someone to blame.

"I can't talk today, Terence," she snapped. She turned toward a pile of baking tins that needed repair and tugged at her fringe. "I have a lot of work, and I'm already behind."

"Oh." Terence's shoulders sagged. "Just

let me know if you need anything," he said, and headed for the door. "Bye, Tink."

As soon as Terence was gone, Tink flew to a nearby birch tree where a carpenter-talent sparrow man worked and asked if she could borrow his hammer. The sparrow man agreed, provided that she brought it back in two days' time. He was in the middle of cutting oak slats for some repairs in the Home Tree, he said, and wouldn't need the hammer until he was through. Tink promised she would.

Two days. Tink didn't know what she'd do after that. But she wasn't going to think about it, she decided. Not just yet.

When Tink entered her empty workshop, something seemed different. There was a sweet smell in the air. Then she spied a plate with a pumpkin muffin on it and a cup of buttermilk on her workbench.

Terence, Tink thought. She was sorry that she'd snapped at him earlier.

The muffin was moist, sweet, and still warm from the oven, and it melted on her tongue. The buttermilk was cool and tart. As soon as she'd eaten, Tink felt better.

She picked up the carpenter's hammer and began to work on a stack of pie pans. The pans weren't cracked or dented, but Dulcie, the baking-talent fairy who'd brought them to her, complained that the pies she baked in them kept burning. Tink thought it had something to do with the pans' shape, or maybe the tin on the bottom of the pans was too thin.

The carpenter's hammer was almost twice as big as her tinker's hammer.

Holding it in her hand, Tink felt as clumsy as a Clumsy.

Still, she had to admit that it was much better than the pebble.

Tink worked slowly with the awkward hammer. She reshaped the pie pans, then added an extra layer of tin to the bottom of each one. When she was done, she looked over her work.

It's not the best job I've ever done, she thought. *But it's not so bad, either.*

Tink gathered the pie pans into a stack and carried them to Dulcie. Dulcie was delighted to have them back.

"Don't miss tea this afternoon, Tink," she said with a wink as she brushed flour from her hands. "We're making strawberry pie. I'll save you an extra-big slice!"

On the way back to her workshop,

Tink ran into Prilla, a young fairy with a freckled nose and a bouncy nature. Prilla always did cartwheels and handsprings when she was excited about something.

"Tink!" Prilla cried, bounding over to her. "Did you hear?"

"Hear what?" asked Tink.

"About Queen Ree's tub," Prilla told her. Ree was the fairies' nickname for their queen, Clarion. "It's sprung a leak. The queen's whole bath trickled out while she was washing this morning."

Tink's eyes widened. The bathtub was one of Queen Ree's most prized possessions. It was the size of a coconut shell and made of Never pewter, with morning glory leaves sculpted into its sides. The tub rested on four feet shaped like lions' paws, and there were two notches at the back where the queen could rest her wings to keep them dry while she took her bath.

Tink's fingers twitched. She would love to work on the bathtub.

"The queen's attendants looked all over, but they couldn't spot the leak. I thought of you when I heard, Tink," Prilla said. "Of course, Queen Ree will want you to fix it. You're the best." Prilla grinned at Tink and did a handspring.

Tink grinned back, showing her deep dimples. It was the first time she'd smiled since she lost her hammer. "I hope so, Prilla. It would be quite an honour to work on the queen's tub," she replied.

Prilla turned a one-handed cartwheel and flew on. "See you later, Tink!" she called.

Tink thought about the queen's tub all afternoon as she fixed the spout on a tea-kettle that wouldn't whistle. What kind of leak could it be? A hairline crack? Or a pinprick hole? Tink smiled, imagining the possibilities.

By the time Tink had finished fixing the kettle, it was nearly teatime.

"They'll need this in the kitchen," Tink said to herself as she buffed the tea kettle with a piece of suede. She would take it to the kitchen, then go to the tearoom for strawberry pie. Tink's stomach rumbled hungrily at the thought. Strawberry was one of her favourite kinds of pie.

But when she got to the kitchen, a horrible smell greeted her. Tink quickly handed the teakettle to one of the cooking-talent fairies and held both hands to her nose. "What is that smell?" she asked the fairy. "It's not strawberry pie."

But the fairy just gave her a strange

look and hurried off to fill the teakettle with water.

Tink made her way through the kitchen until she found Dulcie. She was standing over several steaming pies that had just been pulled from the oven. She looked as if she might cry.

"Dulcie, what's going on?" Tink asked.

As soon as Dulcie saw Tink, her forehead wrinkled. The wrinkles made little creases in the flour on her skin, which made the lines seem even deeper.

"Oh, Tink. I don't know how to tell you this," Dulcie said. "It's the pies. They're all coming out mincemeat."

Tink turned and looked at the steaming pies. That was where the horrible smell was coming from.

"We tried everything," Dulcie went on.

"When the strawberry came out all wrong, we tried plum. When that didn't work, we tried cherry. We even tried pumpkin. But every time we pulled the pies out of the oven, they'd turned into mincemeat." Now Dulcie's chin wrinkled like a walnut as she struggled to hold back tears. Her whole face was puckered with worry.

This was indeed a kitchen disaster. Fairies hate mincemeat. To them it tastes like burned broccoli and old socks.

"Is there something wrong with the oven?" Tink asked Dulcie. She didn't know much about ovens. But if there was something metal in it, she could probably fix it.

Dulcie swallowed hard.

"No, Tink," she said. "It's the pans you fixed. Only the pies baked in those pans are the ones that get spoiled."

5

TINK'S MIND REELED. She took a step back from Dulcie. But before she could say anything, a shrill whistle split the air.

The tea water had boiled. A cooking-talent sparrow man hurried over to lift the kettle off the fire. Expertly, the sparrow man poured the water into the teacups until there wasn't a drop left.

But the teakettle continued to shriek. The sparrow man lifted the kettle's lid to let out any steam that might have been caught inside. A puff of steam escaped, but the kettle still whistled on. Without pausing, it changed pitch and began to whistle a lively, earsplitting melody.

All the fairies in the kitchen, including Tink, covered their ears. Several fairies from other talents who were in the tearoom poked their heads in the door of the kitchen.

"What's all that noise?" a garden-talent fairy asked one of the baking-talent fairies.

"It's the teakettle, the one that just wouldn't whistle," the baking-talent fairy replied. She winced as the kettle hit a particularly high note. "Tink fixed it, and now it won't shut up!"

Twee-twee-tweeeeeeeeee! the teakettle shrieked cheerfully, as if confirming that what she'd said was true. The fairies cringed and clamped their hands more tightly against their ears.

"And the pie pans Tink fixed aren't any good, either," another baking-talent fairy noted over the noise. "Every pie baked in them turns into mincemeat!"

A murmur went around the room. What could this mean? the other fairies wondered. Was it some kind of bad joke? Everyone turned and looked at Tink.

Tink stared back at them, blushing so deeply her glow turned orange. Then, without thinking, she turned and fled.

Tink was sitting in the shade of a wild rosebush, deep in thought. She didn't notice Vidia, a fast-flying-talent fairy, flying overhead. Suddenly, Vidia landed right in front of Tink.

"Tinker Bell, darling," Vidia greeted her.

"Hello, Vidia," Tink replied. Of all the fairies in the kingdom, Vidia was the one Tink liked the least. Vidia was pretty, with her long dark hair, arched eyebrows, and pouting lips. But she was selfish and mean-spirited, and at the moment she was smiling in a way Tink didn't like at all.

"I'm so *sorry* to hear about your trouble, Tink darling," Vidia said.

"It's nothing," Tink said. "I was just flustered. I'll go back to the kitchen and fix the teakettle now."

"Oh, don't worry about that. Angus was in the tearoom," Vidia said. Angus was a pots-and-pans sparrow man. "He got the teakettle to shut up. No, Tink, what I meant was, I'm sorry to hear about your *talent*."

Tink blinked. "What do you mean?"

"Oh, don't you know?" Vidia asked. "Everyone's talking about it. The rumour flying around the kingdom, Tink dear, is that you've lost your talent."

"What?" Tink leaped to her feet.

"Oh, it's such a *shame*, dearest," Vidia went on, shaking her head. "You were always such a good little tinker."

"I haven't lost my talent," Tink growled. Her cheeks were burning. Her hands were balled into fists.

"If you say so. But, sweetheart, you have to admit, your work hasn't exactly been... *inspired* lately. Why, even I could fix pots and pans better than that," Vidia said with a little laugh. "But I wouldn't worry too much. I'm sure they won't make you leave the fairy kingdom *forever*, even if your talent has dried up for good."

Tink looked at her coldly. *I wish* you *would leave forever*, she thought. But she wasn't going to give Vidia the satisfaction of seeing that she was mad. Instead, she said, "I'm sure that would never happen, Vidia."

"Yes." Vidia gave Tink a pitying smile. "But no one really knows, do they? After all, no fairy has ever lost her talent before. But I guess we'll soon find out. You see, dear heart, I've come with a message. The queen would like to see you."

Tink's stomach did a little flip. The queen?

"She's in the gazebo," Vidia told her. "I'll let you fly there on your own. I expect you'll want to collect your thoughts. Goodbye, Tink." With a last sugary smile, Vidia flew away.

Tink's heart raced. What could this mean? Was it really possible that she could be banished from the kingdom for losing her talent?

But I haven't lost my talent! Tink thought indignantly. *I've just lost my hammer.*

With that thought in mind, Tink took a deep breath, lifted her chin, and flew off to meet the queen.

6

AS SHE MADE her way to the gazebo, Tink passed a group of harvest-talent fairies filling wheelbarrows with sunflower seeds to take to the kitchen. They laughed and chatted as they worked, but as soon as they saw Tink, they all stopped talking. Silently, they watched her go by. Tink could have sworn she heard one of them whisper the word "talent."

So it's true, Tink thought. *Everyone is saying I've lost my talent.*

Tink scowled as she flew past another group of fairies who silently gawked at her. She had always hated gossip, and now she hated it even more.

The queen's gazebo sat high on a rock overlooking the fairy kingdom. Tink landed lightly on a bed of soft moss outside the entrance. All around her she heard the jingle of seashell wind chimes, which hung around the gazebo.

Inside, the gazebo was drenched in purple from the sunlight filtering through the violet petals that made up the roof. Soft, fresh fir needles carpeted the floor and gave off a piney scent.

Queen Ree stood at one of the open windows. She was looking out at the glittering blue water of the Mermaid Lagoon, which lay in the distance beyond the fairy kingdom. When she heard Tink, she turned.

"Tinker Bell, come in," said the queen.

Tink stepped inside. She waited.

"Tink, how are you feeling?" Queen Ree asked.

"I'm fine," Tink replied.

"Are you sleeping well?" asked the queen.

"Well enough," Tink told her. *Except for last night*, she added to herself. But she didn't feel the need to tell this to the queen.

"No cough? Your glow hasn't changed colour?" asked the queen.

"No," Tink replied. Suddenly, she realised that the queen was checking her for signs of fairy distemper. It was a rare illness, but very contagious. If Tink had it, she would have to be separated from the group to keep from making the whole fairy kingdom sick. "No, I'm fine," Tink repeated to reassure her. "I feel very well. Really."

When the queen heard this, she

seemed to relax. It was just the slightest change in her posture, but Tink noticed, and she, too, breathed a sigh of relief. Queen Ree would not banish her, Tink realised. The queen would never make such a hasty or unfair decision. It had been mean and spiteful of Vidia to say such a thing.

"Tink, you know there are rumours..." Queen Ree hesitated. She was reluctant to repeat them.

"They say I've lost my talent," Tink said quickly so that the queen wouldn't have to. "It's nasty gossip – and untrue. It's just that – " Tink stopped. She tugged at her fringe.

She was afraid that if she told Queen Ree about her missing hammer, the queen would think she was irresponsible.

Queen Ree waited for Tink to go on. When she didn't, the queen walked closer to her and looked into her blue eyes. "Tink," she said, "is there anything you want to tell me?"

She asked so gently that Tink felt the urge to plop down on the soft fir needles and tell her everything – about the pebble hammer and the carpenter's hammer and even about Peter Pan. But Tink had never told another fairy about Peter, and she was afraid to now.

Besides, Tink told herself, *the queen has more important things to worry about than a missing hammer.*

Tink shook her head. "No," she said. "I'm sorry my pots and pans haven't been very good lately. I'll try to do better."

Queen Ree looked carefully at her. She

knew something was wrong, but she didn't know what. She only knew that Tink didn't want to tell her. "Very well," she said. As Tink turned to leave, she added, "Be good to yourself, Tink."

Outside, Tink felt better. The meeting with the queen had been nothing to worry about at all. Maybe things weren't as bad as they seemed. *All I have to do now is find a new hammer, and everything will be back to normal,* Tink thought with a burst of confidence.

"Tink!" someone called.

She looked down and saw Rani and Prilla standing knee-deep in a puddle. Tink flew down and landed at the edge.

"What are you doing?" she asked, eyeing the fairies' wet clothes and hair. She was used to seeing Rani in the water. But Prilla wasn't a water fairy.

"Rani's showing me how she makes fountains in the water," Prilla explained. "I want to learn. I thought it might be fun to try in Clumsy children's lemonade." Prilla's talent was travelling over to the mainland in the blink of an eye and visiting the children there. She was the only fairy in all of Never Land who had this talent, and it was an important one. She helped keep up children's belief in fairies, which in turn saved the fairies' lives.

Tink looked at the drenched hem of Prilla's long dress and shivered. She didn't like to get wet – it always made her feel cold. She was surprised that Prilla could stand to be in the water for so long.

"I've been trying all afternoon, but this is all I can do," Prilla told her. She took a pinch of fairy dust and sprinkled it onto the water. Then she stared hard at the spot where the dust had landed and concentrated with all her might. After a moment, a few small bubbles rose to the surface and popped.

"Like a tadpole burping," Prilla said with a sigh. "Now watch Rani."

Rani sprinkled a pinch of fairy dust on the water, then stared at the spot where it had landed. Instantly, a twelve-inch fountain of water shot up from the puddle.

Tink and Prilla clapped their hands and cheered. "If I could make just a teeny little fountain, I'd be happy," Prilla confessed to Tink. Tink nodded, though she didn't really understand. She'd never wanted to make a water fountain.

Just then, Tink heard a snuffling sound. She turned and saw that Rani was crying.

"I'm so sorry, Tink," Rani said. She pulled a damp leafkerchief from one of her many pockets and blew her nose into it. As a water fairy, Rani cried a lot and was always prepared. "About your talent, I mean."

Tink's smile faded. She tugged at her fringe. "There's nothing to be sorry about. There's nothing wrong with my talent," she said irritably.

"Don't worry, Tink," Prilla said. "I know how you feel. When I thought I didn't have a talent, it was awful." Prilla hadn't known what her talent was when she first arrived in Never Land. She'd had to figure it out on her own. "Maybe you just need to try lots of things," she advised Tink, "and then it will come to you."

"I already have a talent, Prilla," Tink said carefully.

"But maybe you need another talent, like a backup when the one you have isn't working," Prilla went on. "You could learn to make fountains with me. Rani will teach you, too, won't you, Rani?"

Rani sniffled helplessly. Tink tugged her fringe so hard that a few blonde hairs came out in her fingers. What Prilla was suggesting sounded crazy to Tink. She had never wanted to do anything but fix pots and pans.

"Anyway, Tink," said Prilla, "I wouldn't worry too much about what everyone is saying about – "

"Dinner?" Rani cut Prilla off.

Prilla looked at her. "No, I meant – "

"Yes, about dinner," Rani interrupted again, more firmly. She had dried her eyes and now she was looking hard at Prilla. Rani could see that the topic of talents was upsetting Tink, and she wanted Prilla to be quiet. "It's time, isn't it?"

"Yes," said Tink. But she wasn't looking at Rani and Prilla. Her mind seemed to be somewhere else altogether.

Rani put her fingers to her mouth and whistled. They heard the sound of wings beating overhead. A moment later, Brother Dove landed on the ground next to Rani. He would take her to the tearoom.

But before Rani had even climbed onto his back, Tink took off in the direction of the Home Tree without another word. Rani and Prilla had no choice but to follow.

WHEN THEY REACHED the tearoom, Tink said goodbye to Rani and Prilla. Rani was going to sit with the other water-talent fairies, and Prilla was joining her. Since Prilla didn't have her own talent group, she was an honorary member of many different talents, and she sat at a different table every night. Tonight she would sit with the water-talent fairies and practice making fountains in her soup.

Tink made her way over to a table under a large chandelier where the pots-and-pans fairies sat together for their meals. As she took her seat, the other fairies at the table barely looked up.

"It's a crack in the bottom, I'll bet," a fairy named Zuzu was saying. "I mended a pewter bowl once that had had boiling water poured in it when it was cold. A crack had formed right down the centre." Her eyes glazed over happily as she recalled fixing the bowl.

"But don't you think it could be something around the drain, since the water leaked out so quickly?" asked Angus, the sparrow man who had fixed the whistling teakettle in the kitchen earlier that day.

A serving-talent fairy with a large soup tureen walked over to the table and began to ladle chestnut dumpling soup into the fairies' bowls. Tink noticed with pride that the ladle was one she had once repaired.

She leaned forward. "What's everyone talking about?" she asked the rest of the table.

The other fairies turned, as if noticing for the first time that Tink was sitting there.

"About Queen Ree's bathtub," Zuzu explained. "She's asked us to come fix it tomorrow. We're trying to guess what's wrong with it."

"Oh, yes!" said Tink. "I've been thinking about that, too. It might be a pinprick hole. Those are the sneakiest sorts of leaks – the water just sort of drizzles out one drop at a time." Tink laughed.

But no one joined her. She looked around the table. The other fairies were staring at her, or looking awkwardly down at their soup bowls. Suddenly, Tink realised that the queen had said nothing to her about the bathtub that afternoon in the gazebo.

"Tink," another fairy named Copper said gently, "we've all agreed that Angus and Zuzu should be the ones to repair the tub, since they are the most talented pots-and-pans fairies... lately, that is."

"Oh!" said Tink. "Of course." She swallowed hard. She felt as if a whole chestnut dumpling were stuck in her throat.

Now all the pots-and-pans fairies were looking at Tink with a mixture of love and concern. And, Tink was sad to see, pity.

I could just tell everyone that I lost my hammer, Tink thought. *But if they asked about the spare…*

Tink couldn't finish the thought. For a long, long time, Tink had neglected her pots and pans to spend all her time with Peter Pan. It was something she thought the other pots-and-pans fairies would never understand.

At last the fairies changed the topic and began to talk about the leaky pots and broken teakettles they'd fixed that day. As they chattered and laughed, Tink silently ate her soup.

Nearby, a cheer went up from the water fairies' table. Tink looked over and saw that Prilla had succeeded in making a tiny fountain in her soup.

Prilla has two talents now, Tink thought glumly. *And I haven't even got one.*

As soon as she was done with her soup, Tink put down her spoon and slipped away from the table. The other pots-and-pans fairies were so busy talking, they didn't notice her leaving.

Outside, Tink returned to the topmost branches of the Home Tree, where she'd sat the night before. She didn't want to go back to her workshop – there were pots and pans still waiting to be fixed. She didn't want to go to her room, either. It seemed too lonely there. At least here she had the stars to keep her company.

"Maybe it's true that I've lost my talent," Tink said to the stars. "If I don't have a hammer, then I can't fix things. And if I can't fix things, it's just like having no talent at all."

The stars only twinkled in reply.

From where she was sitting, Tink could see the hawthorn tree where Mother Dove lived. Between its branches, she could make out the faint shape of Mother Dove's nest. Mother Dove was the only creature in the fairy kingdom who knew all about Tink and Peter Pan. Once, after the hurricane that broke Mother Dove's wings and nearly destroyed Never Land, Tink had sat on the beach with Mother Dove and told her tales of her adventures with Peter. She had also told Mother Dove about the Wendy, and how when she came to Never Land, Peter forgot all about Tink.

What a comfort it would be to go to Mother Dove. She would know what to do.

But something held Tink back. She remembered Mother Dove's words to her on her very first day in Never Land: *You're Tinker Bell, sound and fine as a bell. Shiny and jaunty as a new pot. Brave enough for anything, the most courageous fairy to come in a long year.* Tink had felt so proud that day.

But Tink didn't feel very brave right now, certainly not brave enough to go to Peter's and get her spare hammer. He was only a boy, but still she couldn't find the courage.

Tink couldn't bear the idea that Mother Dove would think she wasn't brave or sound or fine. It would be worse than losing her talent.

"Tink," said a voice.

Tink turned. Terence was standing behind her on the branch. She'd been so wrapped up in her thoughts, she hadn't even heard him fly up.

"I haven't fixed the ladle yet," Tink told him miserably.

"I didn't come because of the ladle," Terence replied. "I saw you leave the tearoom."

When Tink didn't explain, Terence sat down next to her on the branch. "Tink, are you all right? Everyone is saying that... " He paused. Like Queen Ree, Terence couldn't bring himself to repeat the gossip. It seemed too unkind.

"That I've lost my talent," Tink finished for him. She sighed. "Maybe they're right, Terence. I can't seem to fix anything. Everything I touch comes out worse than when I started."

Terence was startled. One thing he had always admired about Tink was her fierceness: her fierce dark eyebrows, her fierce determination, even the fierce happiness of her dimpled smile. He had never seen her look as defeated as she did now.

"I don't believe that," he told her. "You're the best pots-and-pans fairy in the kingdom. Talent doesn't just go away like that."

Tink said nothing. But she felt grateful to him for not believing the rumours. For still believing in her.

"Tink," Terence asked gently, "what's really going on?"

Tink hesitated. "I lost my hammer," she blurted at last.

As soon as the words left her lips, Tink felt relieved. It was as if she'd let out a huge breath that she'd been holding in.

"Is that all it is?" Terence said. He almost laughed. It seemed like such a small thing. "But you could borrow a hammer," he suggested.

Tink told Terence about the hammer she'd made from a pebble and the one she'd borrowed from the carpenter fairy. "Neither of them works," she explained. "I need a tinker's hammer."

"Maybe there's a spare – " Terence began.

"I *have* a spare," Tink wailed. She'd already been over this so many times in her own mind. "But it's... I... I left it at Peter Pan's hideout."

"He won't give it back?" asked Terence.

Tink shook her head. "I haven't asked." She looked away.

Terence didn't know much about Peter Pan, only that Tink had been friends with him and then – suddenly – she wasn't. But he saw that Tink was upset and ashamed, and he didn't ask her anything more. Again, Tink felt a surge of gratitude toward him.

They sat silently for a moment, looking up at the stars.

"I could go with you," Terence said at last. "To Peter Pan's, I mean."

Tink's mind raced. Perhaps if someone

else came along, it wouldn't be so hard to see Peter...

"You would do that?" she asked.

"Tink," said Terence, "I'm your friend. You don't even need to ask."

He gave Tink a sparkling smile. This time, Tink saw it and she smiled back.

8

EARLY THE NEXT morning, before most of the fairy kingdom was awake, Tink rapped at the door of Terence's room. She wanted to leave for Peter's hideout before she lost her nerve altogether.

Terence threw open the door after the first knock. He grinned at Tink. "Ready to go get your talent back, Tinker Bell?"

Tink smiled. She was glad Terence was going with her, and not just because it would be easier with someone else along.

They left Pixie Hollow just as the sun's rays shone over Torth Mountain. They flew over the banana farms, where the Tiffens were already out working in the fields. In the distance, they could hear the laughter of the mermaids in the lagoon.

"See that peak?" Tink told Terence. She pointed out a chair-shaped spot at the top of a hill. "That's called the Throne. When the Lost Boys have their skirmishes, the winner is named king of the hill. Of course, if Peter is there, he always wins. The Lost Boys wouldn't dare to beat him, even if they could," Tink explained.

"And that stream," she went on, pointing to a silver ribbon of water winding through the forest below, "leads to an underground cavern that's filled with gold and silver. Captain Hook and his men have hidden away a whole pirate ship's worth of treasure there."

Tink remembered how she had found the cavern. She had been racing along the stream in a little birchbark canoe Peter had made for her. Peter had been running along the bank. When the stream suddenly dove underground, Tink had plunged right along with it. Peter had been so thrilled with her discovery that Tink hadn't even minded the soaking she got when the canoe splashed down in the cavern.

"You must know Never Land better than any fairy in the kingdom," Terence said admiringly.

Tink looked at the island below her and felt a little twinge of pride. What Terence said was true. With Peter, Tink had explored nearly every inch of Never Land. Every rock, meadow, and hill reminded her of some adventure.

Of course, they also reminded her of Peter.

Tink felt a flutter of nervousness. How would it be to see him? What if the

Wendy was there, or Peter had found someone else to play with? What if he ignored her again?

Tink fell silent. Terence, sensing that something bothered her, said nothing more for the rest of their trip.

When Tink reached the densest, darkest part of the forest, she began to glide down in a spiral. Terence followed her.

They plunged through a canopy of fig trees and landed on a white-speckled mushroom. The mushroom was nearly as wide as a Clumsy's dinner plate. Terence was surprised to feel that it was quite warm.

"It's Peter's hideout," Tink explained. "They use a mushroom cap to disguise the chimney to fool Captain Hook."

After they'd rested for a moment, Tink sprang from the mushroom and flew up to a hollow in the trunk of a nearby jackfruit tree. She was about to dive inside when Terence grabbed her wrist.

"What about owls?" he said worriedly. If there was an owl living in the hollow, it might eat them.

Tink laughed. "Anything that lived here would be terrorised by the Lost Boys. This is the entrance to the hideout!"

Peeking inside, Terence saw the entire tree was hollow, right to its roots. He followed Tink as she flew down the trunk. They came out in an underground room.

Terence looked around. The floor and walls were made of packed earth. Tree roots hung down from the ceiling, and from these, string hammocks dangled limply. Here and there on the ground lay slingshots, socks, and dirty coconut-shell bowls. The remains of a fire smoldered in a corner. The whole place had the dry, puppyish smell of little boys.

But there were no little boys in sight. The hideout was empty.

He's not home, Tink thought. She felt both disappointed and relieved.

Just then, they heard whistling coming from somewhere near the back of the den.

Tink and Terence flew toward the sound. Their glows made two bright spots of light in the dim room.

At the back of the hideout, they spied a nook that was tucked out of sight from the rest of the room. The whistling was coming from there.

When they rounded the corner, Terence saw a freckled boy with a mop of red hair sitting on a stool formed by a thick, twisted root. In one hand he held a jackknife, and he whistled as he worked it over a piece of wood. A fishing pole leaned against the wall behind him. Looking more closely, Terence saw that the boy was carving a fishing hook big enough to catch a whale.

Tink saw her old friend, Peter Pan.

Taking a deep breath, Tink said, "Hello, Peter."

But Peter didn't seem to hear her. He continued to whistle and chip at the wood.

Tink flew a little bit closer. "Peter!" she exclaimed.

Peter kept on whistling and whittling.

Was he deaf? Or could he be angry with her? Tink wondered with a sudden shock. The thought had never occurred to her. She hovered, unsure what to do.

Then Terence took her hand. They

flew up to Peter until they were just a few inches from his face. "Peter!" they both cried.

Peter lifted his head. When he saw them, a bright smile lit his face.

Tink smiled, too.

"Hello! What's this?" Peter said. He looked back and forth between the fairies. "Two butterflies have come to visit me! Are you lost, butterflies?"

Tink's smile faded. She and Terence stared at Peter. *Butterflies?*

Tink thought, *Has he forgotten me already?*

Peter squinted at them and whistled low. "You're awful pretty. I just love butterflies," he said. "You'd make a fine addition to my collection. Let's see now, where are my pins?"

He began to search his pockets. As he did, small items fell onto the ground beneath his seat: a parrot's feather, a snail shell, a bit of string.

"Here it is!" he cried. He held up a straight pin with a coloured bulb on the end. It was big enough to skewer a butterfly – or a fairy – right through the middle.

"Now hold still," Peter said. Gripping the pin in one hand, he reached up to grab Tink and Terence with the other.

"Fly!" Terence screamed to Tink.

Just before Peter's stubby fingers closed around them, the fairies turned and fled toward the exit.

9

BUT AS THEY reached the roots of the jackfruit tree, they heard a whoop of laughter behind them.

Tink stopped and glanced back over her shoulder. Peter was clutching his stomach and shaking with laughter.

"Oh, Tink!" he gasped. "You should have seen the looks on your faces. Butterflies! Oh, I am funny. Oh, oh." He bent over as another round of laughter seized him.

Terence, who had been just ahead of Tink, also stopped and turned. Frowning, he came to hover next to her. He had never met Peter Pan face to face before, and he was starting to think that he wasn't going to like him very much.

But Tink was smiling. It had only been a joke! Peter *did* remember her!

At last Peter stopped laughing. He bounded up to Tink and Terence, his eyes shining.

"Tink!" he cried. "It's awful great to see you. Where've you been hiding?"

"Hello, Peter," Tink replied. "Meet my friend Terence."

"A boy pixie! Fantastic!" Peter cried, turning to stare at Terence.

The grin on his face was so wide and enthusiastic that Terence's heart softened. The thing was, it was impossible not to like Peter Pan. He had the eagerness of a puppy, the cleverness of a fox, and the freedom of a lark – all rolled into one spry, redheaded boy.

"You'll never guess what I've got, Tink.

Come see!" He said it as if Tink had been away for a mere few hours and had now come back to play.

Peter led Tink and Terence over to a corner of the hideout and pulled a wooden cigar box out of a hole in the wall. The word "Tarantula" was burned onto the lid. It was the name of the cigars Captain Hook liked to smoke. Peter had found the empty box on the beach, where Hook had thrown it away.

"I keep my most important things in my treasure chest," Peter explained to Terence, gesturing to the box. "The Lost Boys know better than to go poking around in here."

"Where are the Lost Boys?" Tink asked.

Peter thought for a moment. "They

must still be hiding," he replied finally. "We were playing hide-and-seek in the forest yesterday. But when it was my turn to look, I spotted a bobcat stalking a rabbit. Course, I wanted to see if he caught him, so I followed them. I guess I forgot to go back and look for the boys."

"Do you think they're lost?" Terence asked.

Peter grinned. "Course they're lost! They're the Lost Boys! I'll go find them later." He shrugged, then added, "Anyway, that bobcat never did catch the rabbit."

Peter lifted the lid of the cigar box. "Now..." Reaching inside, he took out a small object. He held it out toward Tink and Terence in the palm of his hand. It was yellowish white and shaped like a triangle, with razor-sharp edges that narrowed to a point.

Tink clasped her hands together. "Oh!" she gasped. "You got it!"

"What is it?" Terence asked.

"A shark's tooth," Peter replied, just a bit smugly. "Isn't it swell? I'm going to put it on a string and make a necklace."

"The first time I met Peter, he was trying to steal a shark's tooth," Tink explained to Terence.

"That's right!" exclaimed Peter. "I'd made a bet with the boys that I could steal a tooth from a live shark. I built a small raft out of birchwood and was paddling out to sea... "

From the way he began, Terence could tell that Peter had told this story many times before, and that he loved telling it.

"I had just paddled beyond the reef,"

Peter continued, "when I felt something bump the underside of my raft."

"The shark?" asked Terence.

Peter nodded. "He was looking for his lunch. But he didn't know that I was looking for him, too!"

"How did you plan to get his tooth?" Terence asked.

"I meant to stun him with my oar, then steal the tooth while he was out cold," said Peter. "But he was bigger than I'd thought, and before I knew it, he'd bitten my little raft right in half! I was sinking fast, and it looked like the end for me, when suddenly I heard a jingling sound over my head. I looked up and there was Tinker Bell. She yelled down at me..."

"'Fly, silly boy!'" Tink and Peter cried together. They laughed, remembering.

"But I didn't know how to fly," Peter told Terence. "So Tink taught me how, right then and there. She sprinkled some fairy dust on me, and before I knew it, I'd zipped up into the air, out of the shark's reach. Boy, was he mad!"

"So, you went back and got the shark tooth this time?" Tink asked Peter, pointing to the tooth in his hand.

Peter shrugged. "Naw. A mermaid gave this to me. But now I'm going to go out and get the whole shark!" He pointed to the fishing pole and the wooden hook he'd been carving.

Tink and Peter both burst out laughing.

Terence smiled, watching them. He felt glad that Tink looked so happy. But it also made him sad. What if she decided to stay here in the forest with Peter?

Tink *was* happy. She had discovered that it wasn't so hard to see Peter, after all! She'd only needed a friend to help her find that out. She saw Terence's smile, and she smiled back at him.

Just then, Tink caught sight of something in the cigar box. Her eyes widened. "My hammer!" she exclaimed.

"I saved it for you, Tink," Peter said proudly. "I knew you'd be back for it."

Tink reached into the box and picked up the hammer. It fit perfectly in her hand. She tapped it lightly into the palm of her other hand, then closed her eyes and sighed. She felt as if she'd come home after a long, long trip.

Then, to Terence's joy and relief, Tink turned to Peter and said, "It's been so good to see you, Peter. But we have to go back to the fairy kingdom now."

Peter looked at her in surprise. "What? Now? But what about hide-and-seek?"

Tink shook her head. She was glad to realize that she didn't want to stay, not for hide-and-seek or anything else. She wanted to get back to Pixie Hollow, back to her pots and pans. That was where she belonged.

Tink flew so close to Peter's face that he had to cross his eyes to see her. She kissed the bridge of his freckled nose. "I'll come back soon to visit," she promised. And she meant it.

Then, taking Terence's hand, she flew back out of the jackfruit tree and into the forest.

10

AS TINK HEADED back to the fairy kingdom with Terence, one last thing was bothering her.

She didn't want all of Pixie Hollow to know about the hammer and her trip to see Peter. Enough hurtful gossip had already spread through the kingdom. Tink didn't want any more.

She wanted to ask Terence if he would keep their trip to Peter's a secret between them. But before she could, he turned to her. "I don't think anyone else needs to know about this trip, do you?" he asked. "You've got your hammer back, and that's what matters."

Tink grinned and nodded. What a good friend Terence was.

"The only thing is," Terence said,

"how will we convince everyone that you have your talent back?"

Tink thought for a moment. "I have an idea," she said.

Putting on a burst of speed, Tink raced Terence all the way back to Pixie Hollow.

When they got to the Home Tree, Tink went straight to Queen Ree's quarters.

One of the queen's attendants opened the door. "Tink, welcome," the attendant said when she saw her.

"I've come to fix the queen's bathtub," Tink told her.

Terence, who was standing behind Tink, grinned. Tink was clever. This was the perfect way to prove that her talent was back. Terence didn't doubt that Tink could fix the tub. She was

But the attendant hesitated. Everyone

177

had heard about Tink and her talent. She wanted to refuse to let Tink fix it.

Just then, Ree stepped forward. She had heard Tink's request. "Come in, Tink," she said.

"I've come to fix your bathtub," Tink repeated to the queen.

Ree looked at Tink. In Tink's blue eyes, she saw a fierce certainty that hadn't been there the day before, when they'd talked in the gazebo.

Ree nodded. "Take Tink to the bathtub," she told her attendant.

The attendant looked startled, but she turned and began to lead Tink away.

Just before Tink left, Terence grabbed her hand. "Good luck," he said.

Tink held up her hammer and gave his hand a squeeze. "I don't need it!" she said.

A
Masterpiece
for
Bess

1

"EVERYBODY! COME TO MY room!"

Tinker Bell flew about the tearoom. In a silvery voice she called out to the fairies and sparrow men gathered around the tables.

Lily and Rosetta, two garden-talent fairies, looked up from their breakfast of elderberry scones.

"What's the hurry, Tink?" asked Lily.

"Bess has just painted my portrait –

and you've got to come and see it!" Tinker Bell urged.

Rosetta and Lily looked at each other in surprise. It wasn't every day that Bess painted a new portrait! What was the occasion? they wondered. But before they could ask, Tink had darted out the tearoom door and into the kitchen.

"Let's go," Rosetta said to Lily. They followed Tink through the Home Tree up to her room.

There the fairies packed themselves in wing to wing, like honeybees in a hive. They could see Bess, in her usual paint splattered skirt, standing at the front of the room. She was hanging a life-size, five-inch painting of Tinker Bell.

"Isn't it amazing?" gushed Tink. She flew up behind Lily and Rosetta and landed with a bounce on her loaf-pan bed.

And indeed it was. Bess's painting was so lifelike, if a fairy hadn't known better, she might have thought there were *two* Tinks in the room. No detail – from the dimples in Tink's cheeks to her woven sweetgrass belt – was overlooked. What Tink loved most about the painting, though, were the gleaming metal objects piled all around her: pots, pans, kettles, and colanders. She felt as if she could almost pull each one out of the painting.

It was a perfect portrait, as everyone could see. Right away the oohs and aahs began to echo off the tin walls of Tink's room.

"It's lovely!" said Lily. "Bess, you've outdone yourself again!"

"You're too kind. Really," Bess said.

Her lemon yellow glow turned slightly tangerine as she blushed. As Pixie Hollow's busiest painter, she was used to praise. But she never tired of hearing it.

"It's just what Tink's room needed," added Gwinn, a decoration-talent fairy. She gazed around Tink's metal-filled room.

"What's the occasion?" asked Rosetta.

"Oh, no occasion, really," said Bess. She brushed her long brown bangs out of her violet eyes. "Tink fixed my best palette knife, and I wanted to do something nice in return."

All around her, the fairies murmured approvingly. Bess felt her heart swell with pride. *This is what art is all about*, she thought. Times like these made her work worthwhile.

"Personally, I don't see what the fuss is for," a thorny voice said above the din. "Honestly, my little darlings, what's so great about a fairy standing still?"

Bess didn't have to turn around. She knew who the voice belonged to – and so did everybody else. Vidia, the fastest – and by far the meanest – of the fast-flying-talent fairies, came forward.

"Oh, Vidia," Tink said with a groan. "You wouldn't know fine art if it flew up and nipped you on the nose."

"Yeah, don't listen to her, Bess," Gwinn called out.

"It's okay," Bess assured them. "Every fairy is welcome to have her own opinion."

But as she looked at the portrait again,

she frowned slightly. It wasn't that Vidia's criticism bothered her. She'd learned long ago to let the spiteful fairy's snide comments roll off her wings like dewdrops. But Vidia's remark had started the wheels in Bess's mind turning.

"You know… ," Bess began.

She searched the room for Vidia. But the fairy had already flown away.

"'You know' what?" asked Tink.

Bess shook her head. She turned to Tink with a sunny grin. "There's a whole day ahead of us!" she said. "I don't know about you fairies, but I've got work to do."

Spreading her wings, she lifted into the air. "Thanks for coming, everyone," she called.

And with a happy wave, Bess zipped off to her studio.

2

NOWHERE ELSE DID Bess feel as content as she did in her studio.

Most of the art-talent fairies had studios in the lower branches of the Home Tree. But to Bess there never seemed to be quite enough light – or privacy – there to get her work done. Instead, she had made her studio in an old wooden tangerine crate that had washed up onto a shore of Never Land. She had moved the crate (using magic, of course) to the sunniest, most peaceful corner of Pixie Hollow. It had been her home away from home ever since.

Over time, she'd added things to the crate: a birch-bark cabinet to keep her canvases dry, a soapstone sink in which to wash her brushes, and even a twig cot with a thick hummingbird-down quilt to sleep on when she was painting late into the night.

Bess's studio had grown more and more cluttered. It was, in fact, a bit of a mess. She was not one for tidying up. Why put things away, she always wondered, when you were sure to have to pull them out again someday?

As soon as she reached her studio, Bess began to mix her paints. She took a jar of fragrant linseed oil down from a shelf. Next she brought out a gleaming cherrywood box. The box was polished to a mirrorlike shine. Bess's name was carved into the lid. A carpenter-talent fairy had given it to her as a gift many years before. It was still one of her most prized possessions.

Bess lifted the top of the box. She looked down at the rainbow of powdered pigments inside. Of all the things in her studio, these were the ones she treated like gold.

"Hmm," she mused out loud. "Which colours should I mix first? Orange? Indigo? Hmm… What is that *smell*?"

Following her nose, Bess turned to find two brown eyes peeking in at her through the slats in the tangerine crate.

"Dulcie?" she said in suprise. "Is that you?"

Visitors to her studio were rare. Bess fumbled with the latch as she opened the door. "What is it?"

"Oh, nothing," said Dulcie sweetly.

"I was just passing through the orchard and thought I'd say hi. Oh! And I thought you might like some poppy puff rolls. Fresh out of the oven!"

Dulcie grinned and held up a basket. She lifted a checked linen cloth off the top. The rich scents of butter and tarragon filled Bess's nose. Her mouth began to water.

"Goodness, Dulcie – your famous rolls. You're really too kind!" said Bess, more surprised than ever.

"I thought you'd be hungry," said Dulcie, handing one to Bess. "Especially after working so hard on Tinker Bell's portrait."

Bess took a bite. "*Mmm*," she said. She closed her eyes and let the flaky layers melt on her tongue. "Delicious,

Dulcie! This is so unexpected – and very nice of you! If there's anything I can do for you, just let me know."

"Well," replied Dulcie, "if you wanted to do a portrait of me, that would be fine! I guess I could even pose for you right now. Why, I could pose with my rolls! What do you think? Should I carry the whole basket or just cradle one in my hand like this?"

Bess swallowed what was left of her roll in one surprised gulp.

"Um… uh… actually," she stammered, "I was just about to… "

"I know!" Dulcie exclaimed. "I'll hold a roll in one hand, and the basket in the other! There! Are you getting this, Bess?"

Bess wiped her buttery hands on her skirt. She hadn't planned to paint another portrait. But how could she refuse? And it certainly was flattering to have such an eager model.

"Okay," Bess said. "Why not? I just need to mix up some paints and pick out my brushes."

Dulcie positively fluttered with glee.

From her box, Bess pulled out jars, each filled with a different colour of paint powder: green, blue, black, gold. She decided to start with the chestnut powder, which was remarkably close to the shade of Dulcie's hair. She poured a small mound onto a piece of glass and added linseed oil. Then she carefully used her palette knife to fold the two together. Soon she had a smooth chocolaty brown paste.

She mixed a few more colours and scooped them onto her palette. Pleased, she pulled a clean paintbrush from her pocket. Then she took a hard look at her model. Bess frowned.

"Dulcie," she said, "I wonder if maybe you could move around a little."

"Move around?" said Dulcie. "But what if I drop my rolls?"

And just then, a knock sounded at the door.

3

BESS OPENED HER DOOR to find an enormous bouquet of flowers. Two dainty feet in violet-petal shoes poked out below.

"Rosetta? Is that you?" Bess asked.

"Yes, it's me," replied a muffled voice from behind the flowers. Rosetta's pretty face peeked out from the side. "I brought you these," she said. With a groan, she heaved the heavy bunch toward Bess.

"Lily of the valley. My favorite! What a nice surprise, Rosetta!" Bess exclaimed.

Bess managed to drop the flowers into her cockleshell umbrella stand. She knocked over a few paint pots and canvases as she did.

"I thought you'd like them." Rosetta

beamed. "In fact, I thought you might enjoy *painting* them. Or perhaps it would be better for you if I posed *with* them! As if I were walking through my garden, you know? Something like this – "

Pointing her nose in the air, Rosetta rose on one toe and struck a dramatic pose. "Luckily, I just had my hair done. Usually it's such a mess. Make sure you get each curl, now. Oh, this is going to look so great in my room!"

Bess was speechless. "Er… "

"What Bess is trying to say," Dulcie called from across the room, "is that we are already in the middle of a painting." She held up her basket of rolls for Rosetta to see. "As we say in the kitchen, 'First fairy to come, first fairy served!' But don't worry. Bess will let you know when she's done with *my* portrait. Won't you, Bess?"

"Er… ," said Bess.

"Oh, I see," Rosetta said. Her delicate wings slumped sadly. "Well, in the meantime, I'll go clear a space back in my room for my new portrait. I know exactly where it should go!" She gave them both a little wave and hurried out.

"Fly safely!" called Dulcie.

Bess closed the door behind Rosetta. She felt extremely flattered – and still a little stunned. It was part of her role as an art talent to do paintings for her fellow fairies. Till that morning, they had always been for special occasions: an Arrival Day portrait, or a new painting for the Home Tree corridor. In between, she was as free as a bird to paint whatever she wanted.

But now, right out of the blue, *two*

fairies wanted their pictures painted in one day! That was a record for any art-talent fairy, Bess was sure.

Bless my wings, she thought. *Who knew that Never fairies had such great taste!*

"Shall we continue?" asked Dulcie.

Bess picked up her brush and nodded. "Of course!"

But within minutes, another knock sounded at the door... then another... and another!

By midday, fifteen fairies had paid Bess a visit, and fourteen wanted their portraits painted. (Terence, a dust-talent sparrow man, had stopped by only to drop off Bess's daily portion of fairy dust and to compliment her on Tinker Bell's portrait.)

Everyone wanted a portrait just like

Tink's. There were so many requests, in fact, that Bess had given up on painting them one at a time. Instead, she had each fairy come in to sit for a sketch. Her plan was to finish the paintings later. But by the fourteenth fairy, even finishing a sketch began to look iffy.

"Fern, it's really hard to sketch you when you keep dusting my paper," Bess said to the dusting-talent fairy hovering over her easel.

"Oops!" said Fern. She darted back to the pedestal Bess had set up for her. "It's a habit," she explained. "But *really*, Bess." She shook her head. "I do wish you'd let a dusting talent in here once in a while! How can you stand it? And now, with all these baskets and flowers… my goodness! It's a forest of dust-catchers!"

It was true. Bess's studio was even more cluttered than usual. Fairies who'd come hoping for portraits had brought gifts. There were berries and walnuts from the harvest-talent fairies, cheeses from the dairy-talent fairies, and baskets upon baskets of goodies from the talents in the kitchen. Then there were more baskets from the grass-weaving talents. Not to mention a bubbling foot-high fountain from Silvermist, the water-talent fairy.

Luckily, not all fairies had come with gifts. Hairdressing, floor-polishing, and window- and wing-washing fairies had come offering their services. One music-talent fairy even played a song she'd written just for Bess. (To Bess's dismay, it was *still* stuck in her head!)

"Oh!" Fern exclaimed suddenly.

"There's a speck on your pencil there! Hold on!" She examined it. "Looks like pollen." Then another grain caught her eye. "Over there by the door! Fairy dust. I'll bet Terence left that one."

Feather duster waving at full speed, Fern darted about the room. Bess tried her best to sketch the fairy in action.

At least this is the last sketch I have to do, Bess told herself. *Then just fourteen portraits to paint…*

Knock-knock-knock.

Bess's stomach did a backflip. *Again?* For a second, she was tempted to pretend that no one was home. But she quickly realized that Fern's darting glow and humming duster had already given them away.

Slowly, Bess opened the door.

"Oh, Quill! It's you!" Bess let out a sigh of relief that even Fern could hear. "You wouldn't believe how many fairies and sparrow men have come to my studio today," she said.

She tried not to sound boastful. But she wanted Quill to know how much the other fairies liked her work. Bess always felt self-conscious around Quill. Perhaps it was because Quill was so unbelievably neat, while Bess was so messy.

"Fourteen!" Bess blurted, unable to hold back. "Everyone wanting portraits! I've never seen anything like it!" she went on. "I mean, just look at all the things they've brought me!" She waved her brush at the piles of gifts. Then suddenly she paused. "You weren't coming to ask for a portrait, too, were you?"

The art-talent fairy shook her head and smiled. "No, I just came by to see if you were ready to go to lunch. I've heard they're serving mushroom tarts and buttercup soup!"

Buttercup soup! Bess hadn't had that in ages, it seemed. *Mmm* – she could taste it already. Then her eyes fell on the pile of sketches on her table.

"I can't." She sighed. "Everyone is counting on me to finish the portraits as soon as I can. I've never seen fairies so passionate about art." She glanced at Quill out of the corner of her eye. "My portrait of Tinker Bell really touched them. *Deeply!* Mushroom tarts and butter-cup soup will simply have to wait."

Bess sighed again. "It's hard to be so important. But I am up to the challenge – and I won't let Pixie Hollow down! Please give the other art talents my greetings, though, won't you, Quill?"

Quill was about to respond when Fern suddenly poked her head out from behind the birch-bark cabinet.

"Did you say buttercup soup?" she asked. "Hang on, Quill. I'm coming with you!"

She flew across the room, swiping at a few dust grains along the way. "Let me know when my portrait's done, Bess. Oooh! I cannot wait to dust it!" she said brightly.

Bess watched the fairies go, and she shut the door behind them. She looked at the sketch she had *tried* to do of Fern. It wasn't perfect, but it was fine for a sketch, she decided. *And it's probably a good idea to start painting now*, Bess thought. *I have a lot to do!*

Filled with a sense of duty, Bess churned out several portraits in the next few hours. But when she started the portrait of Rosetta, the garden-talent fairy – who had *insisted* on wearing her best rose-petal outfit – Bess froze.

Oh, no!

She couldn't believe it. She was all out of red paint! She couldn't finish Rosetta's portrait without it!

There was just one thing to do: go out and get more. This emergency called for berry juice – and lots of it.

Bess picked up a piece of paper and one of her best calligraphy twigs. She wrote a sign and hung it on her door:

Out to get more paint.
Please come back later.

Bess

Then she grabbed one of Dulcie's rolls, along with the first basket she could find, and flew out into the warm afternoon.

4

THE CURRANT ORCHARD was not far from Bess's studio. It was just across Havendish Stream.

Currant juice was a cheerful bright red, which would make fine paint, Bess knew. As she flew toward the fruits, they looked so pretty that Bess had an urge to paint them right then and there. Ah, but how could she? So many fairies were waiting for their portraits. She couldn't disappoint them.

Bess flitted from branch to branch. She piled as many plump currants into her basket as she could carry. A basketful would be – she hoped – enough for now.

She placed one last fruit atop her wobbly pile, then reached out and picked one for herself. If she couldn't paint the currants, at least she could taste them!

She licked her lips, then took a big hungry bite. The sweet red juice dribbled down her chin. Bess watched it fall, drip by drip, onto her skirt. It mixed with paint splatters there.

She swiped at her chin with the back of her hand. *Yes!* she thought with satisfaction. *This colour will do just fine!*

When she was done eating, Bess grabbed hold of the basket's handle. She stretched up her wings, ready to fly away. The heavy basket, however, was not going anywhere. Bess could pick it up – just barely. But she couldn't carry it more than an inch at a time.

She tried unloading a few currants, but it didn't help much. And if she took out too many, she wouldn't have enough to make paint when she got home.

Enviously, Bess watched a bluebird soaring overhead. If only she could speak to animals like an animal-talent fairy, maybe she could get some help. But she couldn't even tell the gnats hovering around to go away. No matter how hard she shooed, they just kept returning.

"Oh, well," Bess said with a sigh. "I guess an inch at a time will have to do."

Bess flew – or hopped, really – out of the orchard and back toward her studio. By the time she reached Havendish Stream, she had settled into a comfortable rhythm: *flap, flap, flap, flap-jump-land. Flap, flap, flap, flap-jump-land.* But the crystal-clear stream stopped her short.

It wasn't that Havendish Stream was

very big; a young deer could have crossed it in a single leap. To a fairy, however, it was huge. And there wasn't a bridge. Fairies usually just flew over the stream.

What am I going to do now? thought Bess. The stream was too wide to hop across. And though she didn't mind getting her feet and legs wet, she didn't want to risk getting her wings wet, too. Water soaked into fairy wings, as into a sponge. And if the stream was deep enough, waterlogged wings could drag her under.

Still, Bess had gotten this far. She wasn't going to give up now!

She thought for a moment. Then she picked up one of the plump currants. With a mighty heave, she tossed it across the stream. The currant landed with a soft bounce on the moss on the other side.

Bess cheered, then reached for another. Soon she was tossing currants across the stream one after the other.

When her basket was empty, Bess lifted it effortlessly and flew across the stream. Then she refilled it and set off hopping once more. She was quite pleased with her clever solution.

"Now to make some paint!"

Back at her studio, Bess dragged a well-worn coconut shell from its resting place against her crate. She set it on the grass next to the back wall and dumped her basketful of currants into it.

Normally, Bess made her paints in small batches. But she'd spent far more time collecting the currants than she'd planned. If she was ever going to get all those fairies their portraits, she'd have to start speeding things up – a lot! That meant making *lots* of paint.

Bess kicked off her shoes and rolled up her spider-silk leggings. Then, ever so carefully, she climbed into the shell.

"Oops!" Bess slipped and almost fell. She caught herself on the shell.

POP! Squish! The pulpy fruit burst out of its skin and oozed coolly between her toes. Bess stomped around in the bowl. Her feet moved faster and faster.

She tried her best to keep her wings high and dry. But she could tell they were growing heavy with juice. *No matter*, she thought. *They'll have plenty of time to dry while I paint.* She looked down at the ruby red juice in the shell. Her heart filled with joy. Without thinking about it, she began to sing…

"*Oh, fairy, fairy, fly with me –* "

"Bess? What are you doing?"

The voice behind Bess took her by surprise. She wavered, and her foot slipped.

Splash!

Bess fell face-first into the sticky red currant mash.

"Bess?"

Slowly, Bess reached for the edge of the shell and pulled herself up. Peeking over the side, she saw Quill's pretty face staring back. In Quill's hands was a tray full of dishes covered with acorn caps.

"Are you all right?" Quill asked.

"Perfectly fine," said Bess. She spit out a bit of currant. "I'm just – uh – making some paint for all my portraits."

Inwardly, Bess groaned. Why did Quill always catch her in her messiest moment?

With as much dignity as she could manage, Bess pulled herself out of the shell. She tumbled to the ground. Covered in bright red juice, she looked as if she had a very bad sunburn.

"I brought you some dinner," Quill said. She set down the tray. "You need a hot meal to keep up your strength."

Even through the currant juice, Bess could smell the rich scents coming from the dishes. She wished, more than anything, that Quill hadn't seen her this way. But it was hard not to be grateful for such a kind gesture.

"I know I'll enjoy it," Bess said.

"Would you like some help washing

your wings?" Quill asked. Her tone was sincere. But Bess caught the corners of her mouth turning up in a smile.

Bess shook her head and blushed. "Oh, no," she assured Quill. "I'll get to that… when I can."

"As you wish," Quill replied. She fluttered her wings and turned back toward the Home Tree.

5

DESPITE HER EMBARRASSMENT, Bess enjoyed the dinner Quill had brought. And she hoped it would give her more energy to work.

But painting wasn't easy. The currant juice quickly dried into a sticky sap. It made Bess's hair and clothes stiff and her wings all but useless.

If I'm ever going to get more painting done, Bess thought, *I'll have to clean myself up.*

She set off toward Havendish Stream again. Her wings were too stiff now for her even to hop, so instead she walked through the meadow. Unfortunately, because fairies hardly ever walked, there were no paths to follow.

Bess climbed through the grass, in and out of a bush, and through a patch of dandelions. By the time she reached the stream, she could hardly move for all the grass and seeds and fluff sticking to her.

She made her way down the mossy bank to the shore. And then she stopped. How was she going to do this?

Bess knew she should have put aside her pride and let Quill help her wash her wings. It wasn't an easy job for any fairy to do by herself. But at the time, Bess had just wanted Quill to leave.

So now the problem was, what if she fell into the water? She had no idea how deep the water was. But she could see that the stream was running at an impish, happy-to-knock-you-over-and-carry-you-away pace.

Cautiously, she dipped in a toe.

"Ooh!" It was cold!

Still, Bess had little choice. It was much too far to walk back to the Home Tree for a proper bath. So she knelt beside the stream. Cupping her hands, she began to splash water onto herself to try to wash the grass and juice away.

The dried juice in her hair was particularly hard to wash out. Finally, she gave up splashing. She leaned over, ready to stick her whole head in the water.

Crrrooaak!

A frog Bess hadn't noticed leaped into the stream. It landed with a splash. Bess didn't have a chance of keeping her balance. The next thing she knew, she fell headfirst into the water, making quite a splash of her own.

"*Sppplugh!*"

She kicked and waved and sputtered, even though her bottom was firmly on the stream's pebbled floor. Luckily, the water was not very deep. Yet the harder Bess flailed, the faster the playful stream became. At last it began to carry her away!

"Stop! Let me out!" Bess begged.

By then her wings were impossibly heavy. "Help!" Bess cried. "Help! Help! *Help!*"

"Bess!" a voice called out. "Stop kicking! The stream doesn't like it! Just calm down, and I'll pull you out. What were you *doing?*"

Bess made herself relax. A second later, her friend Rani, a water-talent fairy, pulled her out of the water. Bess was safe, if sopping, on a sandy shore.

"Rani, you saved me!" Bess panted, as much with exhaustion as with relief. "You must let me do something for you." She tried to raise herself onto her elbows. But her waterlogged wings felt like weights on her back. She settled for rolling over to face her friend. "I know! How about a – "

" – portrait!" Rani almost shrieked. "Just like Tinker Bell's? Bess, you read our minds! We were just talking about how wonderful it would be for each of us to have a portrait!"

"Each of you?" Bess said, confused.

"Yes, each of us!" Rani replied. "Everyone," she called to a group of water-talent fairies. "Come down here and see Bess. She's going to paint portraits of all of us. We'll be the first talent group to have a complete set!" She teared up with joy. "And could somebody please bring me a leafkerchief?" she asked, sniffing loudly.

In seconds, a dozen eager water fairies surrounded Bess.

"So when can you get started?" Rani asked.

"Well, honestly," Bess began, "I have several others to finish first. And then I'll probably have to make more – "

" – paint!" Rani cut in knowingly. "Of course."

"I hope you'll use *watercolors* for all of our portraits," Silvermist said with a giggle. The whole group of water-talent fairies laughed.

Bess managed to smile politely. She struggled to her feet.

"Oh, here, let me help you," said

Rani. "You'll never get anywhere with wings *that* full of water."

She brushed a bit of fairy dust from her arm onto Bess's wings. Then she held her hands above them. Closing her eyes, Rani drew the water out in a thin silvery ribbon. She formed it into a ball and tossed it into the stream.

"Your wings will still be damp for a while," she said, turning back to Bess. "But at least they won't weigh you down."

Bess stood and gave her wings a little flap. "Much better," she said with relief. But her relief turned to dismay as she thought of the new portraits… a whole *talent*'s worth. Goodness!

As she said good-bye to the water fairies, Bess tried to remind herself that portrait painting was an honour.

"Don't forget about our portraits!" the fairies called after her.

"Oh," said Bess, "I won't."

6

BESS HEADED BACK across the meadow, in the direction of her studio. To her dismay, her flying was a little wobbly since her wings were still a bit damp. *But at least I'm clean*, she thought. She tore off a piece of grass and used it to tie back a lock of hair.

With a sigh, Bess realised that she could use some clean clothes. She hadn't been back to her room in the Home Tree in quite a while. A bit of freshening up in general might do her some good. So she quickly turned away from her studio, toward the Home Tree.

As she neared the knothole door, however, her stomach began to churn. Bess's room was in the tree's south-

southwest branch. That meant passing dozens of rooms and workshops. Who knew how many fairies she might meet along the way? And what if they all wanted portraits? Not that Bess didn't want to paint them all. She just wasn't sure she wanted to do it right *now*.

No, going through the Home Tree was *not* the way to get to her room, Bess decided. She would have to sneak in through her back window instead.

Bess had never flown to her room from behind before. But really, how hard could it be? She circled the trunk to the side where the low evening sun was shining. Thank goodness it hadn't set yet! Then she looked up at the rows of brightly coloured window boxes along the tree's branches.

Now, that's a subject for painting, she thought wistfully. But right now, the window boxes were for counting.

"One… two… three… four… five… "

Bess got to thirteen, but then she had to stop. The Home Tree's leafy branches began to block her view. Bess flew closer and continued counting.

"Fourteen… fifteen… sixteen. Here it is!"

Funny, she thought, *I don't remember that leaf in front of my window.*

Bess flew over to the window and tugged on the sash. Stubbornly, it refused to give. She pulled a little harder. But still the window held fast.

"What am I going to do now?" Bess said. She balled her fists and pounded the window in frustration.

Immediately, the window gave way. Bess tumbled inside.

How odd, she thought, shaking her sore head. *I always thought that window opened out...*

"Bess!" came an alarmed voice from across the room. "Are you all right?"

"Quill!" Bess cried, looking up. "What are you doing here?"

"I'm sculpting – in my room," Quill replied. Her voice now sounded more puzzled than shocked.

"*Your* room?" Bess bit her lip as she rose to her feet. Her eyes darted around the tidy chamber. She looked from one stone sculpture to another, over to the cast-bronze bedstead, and then to the marble busts set into each wall. Finally, her eyes went back to Quill.

"Yes," Quill said. "My room. Did you need something, Bess?"

Bess tried to swallow the lump in her throat. She choked out a laugh. "Need something! Ha! That's a good one, Quill. No. No. No. I was just... er... flying by... to let you know I *don't* need anything! And, uh... " She looked down at her limp, wrinkled, stained skirt. "To show you that I cleaned up... all by myself!"

She swallowed once more and stretched her mouth into a grin.

"I see," said Quill. She still looked confused. "I'm... so glad."

"Anyway," Bess went on, "I have portraits of all the water-talent fairies to do. I really must fly off."

"Are you sure I can't help you in

some way?" Quill asked again.

"Absolutely not," said Bess. Still grinning, she took a backward hop toward the door... and ran straight into a granite statue of a luna moth. With a crash it fell from its pedestal onto the hard wooden floor.

Bess cringed. "Oh, no!"

"Don't worry." Quill flew over and sprinkled some fairy dust on the heavy statue. Then she used the magic to stand it back up. "No harm done," she said.

"Truly," said Bess, "I'd fly backward if I could."

Quill laughed. "Flying backward is how you knocked it over in the first place."

Bess knew it was a joke. But she couldn't help noticing that Quill hovered protectively next to the moth statue.

Bess blushed. "See you later, Quill," she said. And she hurried out of the room before she could do more damage.

Oh, of all the rooms to fall into by mistake, why did it have to be Quill's? Bess thought as she flew to the next room down the hall. She reached for the knob. Then, just to be safe, she checked the number on the door to make sure it was hers.

Inside, Bess's mood quickly lifted. It was a relief to be among her favorite things.

She flew to her bed, which was covered in a multi coloured quilt made from different kinds of flower petals. She lay back and gazed up at the stained-glass window above her. The sun was almost down, but there was just enough light to allow the colours to dance along the wall across the room.

And, oh, the walls! They were covered with framed pictures of every shape and size. Many were gifts from other art fairies. The rest were drawings and paintings that Bess had done herself. There was her very first sketch of Mother Dove. Next to it hung her Home Tree series. She'd followed the tree through all its seasons – spring and summer (which were the only seasons in Never Land).

Each work reminded Bess of a time and place and mood. Some were good and some were bad, but each was special in its own way.

Then her eyes fell on a statue in the corner. It was a portrait of Bess carved out of smooth sandalwood. Quill had given it to her as a gift on her last Arrival Day anniversary. Quill had remembered how much more Bess liked wood than hard, cold stone.

Bess smiled at the statue. It was a perfect likeness, right down to Bess's long bangs and the paintbrush behind her ear.

Funny, Bess thought. She yawned and let her heavy eyelids close for just a moment. *If I didn't know better, I'd say that was the work of a good friend.*

7

THE NEXT THING SHE KNEW, Bess awoke to a loud knock at her door. She didn't even remember falling asleep! What time was it?

Knock-knock-knock.

"Bess! Are you in there?"

Groggily, Bess flew up and opened the door.

"Hi, Bess! It's me! Is it done?"

It was Dulcie.

"I went to your studio. Your sign said you'd be there this morning. But when you never showed up, I thought maybe I'd find you here."

"Oh," said Bess. She pushed her hair out of her eyes, trying to wake up.

"*So?*" Dulcie went on. "Is it done?"

"Is what done?"

"My portrait!"

"Oh!" Bess thought for a moment. "As a matter of fact, it is. But it's not here, of course. It's back at my studio."

"Well, come on!" Dulcie grabbed her arm. "Let's go!"

By the time they reached the tangerine crate, Bess was wide awake. She was pleased to be presenting the new portrait.

She had to admit, though, that she was a little disappointed that Dulcie hadn't brought another plate of rolls, or some other tasty treat.

"I came as soon as I woke up!" Dulcie explained excitedly, almost as if she could read Bess's thoughts. "I haven't even been to the kitchen yet to bake."

"Really?" Bess was touched. How important this was to Dulcie! "Let's take a look, then, shall we?" she said.

She led Dulcie to a row of easels, each draped with a thick velvet-moss cloth. With a quick flick of the wrist, and just the right touch of drama and modesty (something every art fairy arrives with), she yanked off the cover of the nearest one.

"Ooh!" Dulcie fluttered up and down. She clapped her hands. "I love it! I love it!" she gushed. "I can practically taste those poppy puff rolls right now!" And as if to test them, she reached out to touch the painting. Then she stopped.

"What? What is it?" asked Bess.

"Do my wings really stick up like that in back?" Dulcie asked. The joy slowly drained from her face.

"What do you mean?" said Bess.

"My wings!" said Dulcie. "They're… *huge*." She strained her neck, trying to see behind herself. "They're not really that big, are they?"

"Actually, they are," came a cheerful voice from just outside the door. "Good morning, Bess. Dulcie. Is my portrait ready, too?"

"Hello, Rosetta," replied Bess. She was still stunned by Dulcie's reaction. "Er, yes. Yours is done, too."

While Dulcie anxiously compared her wings with those in the painting, Bess reached for the second velvet cover and pulled it off.

Rosetta beamed. Then a tiny wrinkle formed between her brows.

"How do you like the lilies of the valley?" Bess asked. "I tried to make each one practically perfect, just like yours, but not so perfect that they wouldn't look real."

"Oh, yes, they're very nice," Rosetta said. Still, she looked concerned. "It's just … my *nose*. I know for a fact that it's much prettier than *that*."

Dulcie glanced away from her portrait. "Actually, it's not."

Rosetta frowned. "Yes, it is. Would you mind, Bess," she went on, "going back and straightening my nose… and maybe taking a little off the sides?"

"Oh, yes!" said Dulcie. "Could you make my wings smaller, too, Bess? That would be wonderful!"

Bess's mouth fell open. Every fairy had her opinions. But Bess had never before been asked to change her art. Like all talents, she prided herself on doing her best from the very beginning. What were these fairies thinking?

But Bess didn't even have time to reply before a dozen more fairies swooped into her studio, each one eager to see her brand-new portrait. And each one, Bess could tell, was eager to offer her honest opinion.

By the time the fairies had left, Bess was drained – and hungry.

She looked at the sun outside her window. It was high in the sky. She had probably missed breakfast by a good hour. But perhaps a few kind serving talents would still be serving tea.

Bess sure hoped so.

As soon as she reached the Home Tree, she flew straight through the lobby and down the long corridor to the tearoom.

She headed directly for the art-talent fairies' table. As she had feared, the other art-talent fairies had finished their breakfast and returned to their own studios. Most of the tables in the tearoom were empty, in fact. The cleaning-talent fairies were busy taking dirty teacups and breakfast trays away.

"Bessy, dear!" called Laidel, a serving-talent fairy. She swooped up beside Bess. "We were afraid you weren't coming. Let me bring you some tea. And maybe a scone?"

"That would be lovely," said Bess, sinking into a chair.

"Coming right up!" said Laidel.

In moments, the fairy was back. Her

tray was piled high with Bess's favourite tea, sweet cream and clover honey, heart-shaped currant – *Ugh!* Bess thought – scones, blueberry muffins with freshly churned butter, and a tall stack of buckwheat pancakes dripping with warm syrup.

"I thought you looked a bit tired, Bess," said Laidel. "So I brought you a little extra." She gave Bess a wink as she poured a stream of tea into a cup. She set it down before Bess. "Don't tell the other fairies!"

Bess smiled at her gratefully and took a sip. "Ahh! Just what I needed."

"I'm so glad," said Laidel. "Now, just sit back, relax, and enjoy your tea. There you go. I'll come back in a little while and we can talk about my portrait."

Pwahhh! Bess's eyes popped open and the tea she'd been sipping sprayed across the tablecloth. Her cup fell to the floor, where the rest of the tea made a stain on the floral carpet.

Bess reached down to mop it up with her napkin. But another hand, clutching a springy moss sponge, beat her to it.

"Allow me," said Colin, a rather tall (in fairy terms) and rather plump (in any terms) cleaning-talent sparrow man. He dabbed at the spill until no trace of tea was left. Then he flew off with the empty cup and returned in an instant with a new one.

"If there's anything else I can do for you, Bess," he said with a bow, "let me know."

"I will," said Bess.

"For instance," Colin went on, "if you'd like me to pose for one of your portraits, just ask. I'm sure you don't come across a model like *me* every day!"

Bess shook her head. "Er, no, I don't," she said. "But to tell you the truth, Colin, I don't need any more models today. I'm a little behind, I'm afraid."

"No problem," Colin said with a shrug. "We'll do it tomorrow." With a smile, he turned. "Hey, Elda!" he called to a cleaning-talent fairy across the room. "I talked to Bess. She says we should come by her studio *tomorrow*!"

Bess poured a new cup of tea. But the joy of the meal had gone away. Not even the buckwheat pancakes (which had always been Bess's favourite) tasted good.

Maybe I should leave, she thought. *I*

should get busy painting again. Besides, who knows how many more portraits I'll have to do if I stay!

But it was too late. Suddenly, a whole line of eager fairies flew out of the kitchen – baking talents, dish-washing talents, silver-polishing talents, serving talents, and everyone else who happened to be around.

"Hi, Bess," called Dulcie. "Colin said you were here. Did you like the scones? I told everyone in the kitchen about my portrait. And don't you know, now they all want one!"

"Oh, yes!" said another baking-talent fairy. "We've each got to have a portrait, too!"

Bess tried not to groan. But it hardly would have mattered if she had. The fairies were busy chattering with each other, describing *exactly* how they wanted their portraits to be.

"Just be sure to keep your wings tucked in," Dulcie said knowingly.

Finally, Bess held up her hands.

"Friends," she began, "I am truly, truly honoured by your regard for my work. But I'm not sure I can paint all your portraits right now. Maybe a quick sketch would do?" she asked hopefully.

The fairies looked at one another.

"No," said one silver-polisher. "We want *portraits*, like everyone else."

"Yes!" the others chimed in. "We want portraits! We want portraits! We want portraits!"

8

BESS LEFT THE TEAROOM with sixteen more portraits to do.

She hoped she'd have enough paint. But as she pulled one, and then another, paintbrush from the pouch at her waist, she realized she would definitely need more brushes.

Vole hair made the best paintbrushes. Bess could usually find patches of it near the edge of the forest. (Those voles just shed like crazy.) The forest was not far from her studio. She decided that she should fly by and collect some on her way.

And she was so glad she did. The light was *gorgeous*! It was streaming through the trees, casting deep, dark shadows that were so… interesting!

Back to business, Bess reminded herself over and over.

But where were all the vole hairs?

Then, at last, just when Bess thought she would have to make do with dandelion fluff, she spotted a tuft of tiny gray hairs stuck to a blade of grass.

She darted over and began to collect them. All of a sudden, she felt a firm, sharp peck on the top of her head!

"Chrrrp-chrrrp! Trillillillillill!"

Bess spun around to see a stern gray bird staring at her. It was twice as big as she was.

"Eeeek!" shrieked Bess.

"Eeeek!" chirped the bird. *"Chrrr-chrrr-chrrrp-trrrillll!"*

A voice rose from the shadows. "She says she needs those hairs for her nest."

Bess looked to the right and saw a reddish brown head poke out from behind a short stump.

"Fawn," Bess said. "I'd fly backward if I could. I didn't know."

"That's okay," Fawn replied. She was an animal-talent fairy. She could talk to animals in their own languages. "These mockingbirds are a little testy. But they don't mean any harm. Just looking out for their babies."

Bess rubbed the sore spot on her head. "I see." She watched the bird pluck the hairs with her beak.

"Do you think she could spare a few hairs for a new paintbrush?" Bess asked Fawn.

Fawn grinned and turned to the bird. Together, they twittered and chirped for a good three or four minutes. Then the fairy turned back to Bess and nodded.

"Take as many as you need," Fawn said.

"That's kind of her!" said Bess. "What in Never Land did you say?"

Fawn grinned again. "I just told her what a fantastic and famous fairy artist you are. And that you needed hairs for a new paintbrush. *And* that if she shared hers, you would paint her portrait!" She winked at Bess and whispered, "She's quite vain, you know. Oh, and I also told her you would paint me, too."

"Paint you?" said Bess.

"Would you?" asked Fawn. "Everyone is talking about your portraits, and I've never had one done. I just saw Madge's. I don't care how much she thinks she looks like a dragonfly – I think it's wonderful! What a great talent you have! Tell me" – Fawn paused and wrapped her arms fondly around the bird – "do you want to paint us here? Or back at your studio?"

"Right now?" Bess said.

"Why not?" said Fawn with a shrug. "It's early. Besides," she went on with a nod toward the mockingbird, "it's the only way you're going to get your vole hairs."

With a halfhearted sigh, Bess sank onto a patch of moss. She pulled some pencils and her sketchbook from her smock. "I'll *sketch* you here," she told the eager pair. "Then I'll paint you back at my studio. *Alone*."

The mockingbird warbled something

to Fawn. "Be sure to paint her right side – it's her best," Fawn translated. "See, what did I tell you? Oh! And when you do me, don't feel as if you have to make my teeth so big, you know? There are some fairies who call me Chipmunk. Can you believe it?"

Bess began her sketch, just as she'd done for all the fairies.

But she soon found her interest drifting away from her models and off to the forest.

The sun slowly shifted across the late-morning sky. A gentle breeze swept up and blew a flock of woolly clouds across the blue horizon. Closer to the forest's edge, shadows shivered and danced about on the ground.

And then, the west wind kicked in.

At first, it was refreshing. But Never winds are fickle and prone to mischief, especially those from the west. And this one was no different.

It began by blowing all the dandelions' fluff off their stalks, leaving their bald-headed stems to flap about. Then it moved into the trees. It worked the leaves into a rustling frenzy. It sent acorns and hickory nuts crashing to the ground.

Feathers flying, the mockingbird did her best to hold her ground – and her good side. Fawn clung to her neck with all her might.

"Uh, Bess! Shall we call it a day?" Fawn hollered over the din.

"Hold on!" Bess called back. She was sketching furiously in her book. "I'm almost done."

"I *can't* hold on!" Fawn cried.

The mockingbird let out a stream of frantic chirps. The wind gleefully carried away half of them. But Fawn understood.

"She has to get back to her nest, Bess," Fawn shouted. "Crazy wind! Her babies are scared!"

Bess sighed. Fawn was right. They all should go. Besides, by now it wasn't easy to keep her sketchbook from blowing away.

She said good-bye to the mockingbird, who swiftly flew off to her chicks. Fawn asked a chipmunk to carry her and Bess home. And off they rode. Bess held her book of sketches tightly. Her heart was full of newfound joy.

Then the wind died away.

BESS COULDN'T WAIT to start painting!

She was bursting with inspiration. Her brushes flew about the canvas.

It wasn't until she stepped back from it that Bess realised that what she had painted wasn't a portrait at all. It was the forest, as she had seen it, in all its pinwheels of texture and color. Great swirls of greens and blues, whites and browns, bright yellows and mysterious grays filled her canvas.

Oh, but it was satisfying! So full of energy and life. Bess hadn't felt this good since she'd finished Tink's portrait. *What's the difference?* she wondered. *What has been missing from all my paintings lately?*

Bess left her studio and flew toward

the Home Tree. On her way, she saw a message-talent fairy. Bess stopped her.

"Do you think you could ask everyone to gather in the courtyard today, just before teatime?" Bess asked her. "The light should be perfect for the unveiling of my newest painting! It's a masterpiece!"

"Of course," the message-talent fairy said, and she quickly flew off.

Bess counted the minutes until teatime. And she couldn't help staring at the masterpiece. Any fairy who appreciated fine painting would absolutely *love* it! She was sure.

Bess's new painting was quite large by fairy standards – five by seven inches. She sprinkled it with fairy dust to make it easier to carry. Then she covered it with a piece of silky cloth and set off for the courtyard of the Home Tree.

Bess had planned on being the first fairy to arrive. But to her surprise, the courtyard was practically full. Everyone was eager to see Bess's great masterpiece.

"It might be a portrait of me!" a dust-talent fairy told a water-talent fairy.

"Or it might be of Fawn," said an animal-talent fairy. "I heard that Bess wouldn't stop sketching her this morning – despite a windstorm!"

"I don't know," someone else said. "It's so large. Perhaps it's *all* of us!"

Finally, it was time. Bess flew up to call everyone to order. Her glow was practically white with excitement.

She smiled at the crowd. "I think you will be glad you flew here today... especially considering what art lovers you all have become! It is because you appreciate art that I couldn't wait to share my newest painting with you. And so… " Bess grabbed the cloth. She yanked it away with a flourish. "I call it… *Swept Away!*"

In the courtyard, there was silence.

Bess looked happily at her painting. Then she turned to her fans. But the faces staring back at her were blank.

"That's not *me*," she heard one or two fairies mumble.

"That's not me, either," echoed several more.

"No, of course!" Bess chuckled. "It's not any of you. It's… it's a feeling I had of being swept away! In the forest… in the moment… in my art! Isn't it wonderful?"

"It's *what?*" she heard Fawn call out.

"It's a feeling," Bess repeated.

Honestly! Bess's forehead wrinkled in frustration. She began to explain once more – but before she could say another word, the tea chimes rang.

"Teatime!" called Laidel.

"We're coming," several fairies cried in reply.

"Very nice, Bess," said a few water-talent fairies politely as they flew by. Bess looked for tears of emotion. But their eyes were surprisingly dry.

The other art-talent fairies applauded her. But even they seemed more eager than usual to make their way inside.

"Wait!" Bess meekly called. Where were all the adoring fairies? Where were all the requests for paintings of their own? Fiddlesticks! Where were all the compliments Bess had... well...

gotten used to?

Within minutes, the courtyard was empty. Bess's glow faded from white to a dull, disappointed mustard color.

She felt her chin begin to tremble. Her eyes welled up with tears.

"Darling, I sincerely hope you're not *crying*. Don't we get enough of that with those pitiful water-talent fairies?"

Bess sniffled and looked up. She saw Vidia flying over.

"I'm not in the mood for your comments right now, Vidia," she managed to say, despite the lump in her throat.

"Suit yourself," said the fairy, turning to go. "I really didn't want to tell you anyway that I liked your painting."

"You *what?*" Bess said with a gasp.

"I like it," replied Vidia, looking back

over her shoulder. "And I'd appreciate it, sweetheart, if you didn't make me say it again."

"Wait!" Bess called out. "Don't go! Stay!" She watched in amazement as the fairy zipped back toward her. "So you really like it?"

Vidia rolled her eyes. "Yes," she said.

Bess grinned. "*Ah*. At least someone does."

"Why, Bess, dear, don't you like it?"

"Well… " Bess stopped to consider Vidia's question. "Yes, I do. I like it very much."

"So there you are. Of course, I can see why you would value *my* opinion. But do you really care so much what those silly slowpokes think?" Vidia scoffed. "Really. And here I thought you were an artist."

It was hard to agree with someone as unpleasant as Vidia. *But she has a point,* Bess thought. Bess loved her painting, and she'd loved painting it. And wasn't that really what art was all about? How could she have let herself forget so easily?

"Um, Vidia," she said. Her hands nervously twisted the cloth that had covered her painting. "Would you, by any chance, like to have this painting?"

For a split second, Vidia actually looked pleased. But her pale face quickly hardened into a scowl. "Darling, are you giving me a present?" she said haughtily. "What in Never Land have I ever done for *you?*"

"You told me the truth," Bess replied. "But more than that, my painting reached you. So I want you to have it."

Vidia's cold eyes moved from Bess to the enormous canvas. And Bess could see them faintly warming.

"I'll take good care of it," Vidia said finally. Then she took a pinch of fairy dust from the pouch hanging from her belt and sprinkled it onto the painting. Picking the painting up, she darted away.

Smiling, Bess watched her go. Then she took a deep breath and braced herself for the difficult task ahead.

10

BESS COULD SMELL the freshly baked honey buns and butter cookies even before she got to the tearoom. But that day, tea would have to wait until after her announcement.

She hated to think about how the other fairies would react. The best thing to do, she told herself, was not think too hard – just do it.

She flew to the front of the great room. She stood between the wide floor-to-ceiling windows and flapped her wings for attention.

"Everyone!" she called. "Everyone! I have an announcement."

The clink of china and the hum of voices, however, did not grow any fainter.

"I *said*," Bess shouted, "I have an

important announcement to make!"

One of her wings accidentally knocked over a tea tray. At last, someone took notice.

"Oh, fairies!" Laidel called out. She clinked a spoon against a cup. "I think Bess has something to say."

The noise died down. All eyes turned to Bess.

"Uh… " Bess was suddenly nervous. How was she going to do this? She wished that she had written her announcement down.

"I… I just wanted to tell you all that I realized something important this morning – something I somehow let myself forget." She brushed her bangs out of her eyes. "The joy of my talent comes not *just* from painting, you see. It comes from painting what *inspires* me, *when* it inspires me. I think that is something you all can understand. I must be true to my talent, and to myself. And so" – Bess drew a deep breath – "although it has been a great honour to be asked to paint so many of your portraits, I won't be able to finish them for quite a while."

Bess closed her eyes. She waited for the backlash.

Clink, clank, slurrrp.

Bess slowly opened one eye, and then the other. All around the room, the fairies had gone back to their tea.

"Wait!" Bess blurted out. "Did you all hear what I said?"

"Oh, yes," several fairies replied.

"We sure did," said a few more.

"You need to be inspired," Laidel

said. "We completely understand."

"I know!" said Dulcie, flying by with a plate of fresh rolls. "Maybe you'd be inspired by Hem's new dress! Stand up, Hem, and show her!"

A plump-cheeked, white-haired fairy modestly stood up. She modelled her frock made of soft pink peony petals. It was tight in the waist and full down to the knees. Hem wore open-toed pink slippers dyed to match. Although Bess liked clothes that were more flowy and colourful, she had to agree that it was very nice.

"Oh, isn't it gorgeous!" cooed Rosetta from the table next to her.

"I've got to have one!" said another garden-talent fairy.

"Me too!" more fairies chimed in.

"Me first, though!" said Dulcie. "Hem promised to make one for me first. Didn't you, Hem? First fairy to come, first fairy served!"

Soon a ring four fairies deep had formed around poor Hem. Teatime – and Bess – had been forgotten.

Bess sank into a nearby chair. She stared, bewildered, at the scene. Could it be that Bess and her portraits had lost all their importance? Had she awakened any real art appreciation in the fairies? Or had her art been just a… just a *fad*?

The idea made her wings limp. Bess's spirits sank. Oh, the horror!

She buried her head in her arms, in case a tear should fall.

"Bess?"

She felt a cool hand on her shoulder.

"Why don't you come to our table?"

Slowly, Bess looked up into Quill's eyes. Her spirits sank even lower. As if making a complete fool of herself weren't bad enough. Did she have to do it right in front of Quill *again*?

"I saved you two star-shaped butter cookies. But if you don't eat them quickly, Linden will."

Bess sniffled a little and shook her head. "I'm not hungry," she said. "I don't know if I'll ever be hungry again."

"Oh, yes, you will," Quill said.

Bess pushed back her bangs. She sniffled once more. "How can you be so sure?"

"Because – " Quill began.

But before she could finish, she was interrupted by Hem's high-pitched voice from the far end of the room. "One at a time, fairies! Please! One at a time!"

Bess and Quill looked over at the ever-widening circle around the dressmaking fairy. They couldn't help smiling at each other.

Quill leaned toward Bess. "Remind me to tell you about the time, a few years before you arrived, when all the fairies decided they just *had* to have their very own tiny hand-carved talent symbols to wear around their necks."

"Really?" Bess was surprised. "That sounds lovely! But... I don't think I've ever seen one."

Quill grinned and nodded. "Exactly."

"*Ah!*" It took a moment, but Bess got it. "Fairies!"

Maybe I will have a cookie or two after

all, Bess thought. And maybe she *would* paint Hem's cute pink dress. Perhaps with a bright green background! Or should it be orange? Or maybe she'd paint something else that day. Or do something with clay? She could even carve with Quill.

There was one thing for sure, though. From then on, whatever Bess did, it would be her choice – and hers alone.

Join Tinker Bell, Prilla and all
the other Never Fairies in
the next Disney Fairies book...

Rani and the
Three Treasures

Here is a fairy-sized preview!

Rani

and the

Three

Treasures

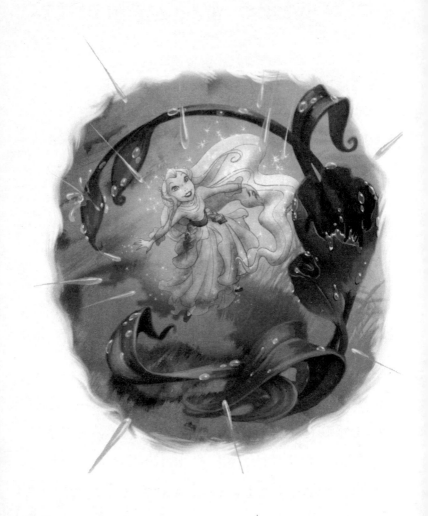

1

"Oh, no!"

Prilla held up her hand and let the water splash into her palm. "Rain! The day is ruined. Hurry, let's get back to the Home Tree before my wings get wet." She fanned her wings and began to lift off from the ground.

Rani took Prilla's hand and tugged her back. "Don't be silly," she said with a laugh. "Rainy days are just as much fun as sunny days."

Prilla frowned. "I don't see how. If your wings get wet, you can't fly. And if you can't fly, then… " Prilla broke off. "Oh, Rani. I'd fly backward if I could. I forgot."

"Don't worry." Rani smiled. She

knew her friend Prilla would never hurt her feelings on purpose. All fairies loved to fly. Rani was the only fairy in Pixie Hollow who couldn't. But Rani wasn't unhappy. She was too full of life.

The rain began to fall faster. Prilla covered her face. She flinched as each heavy drop struck her.

But Rani was a water-talent fairy. To her, every raindrop felt like a kiss. Rani loved the water, and the water loved her.

"Watch this, Prilla!" Rani ran as fast as she could toward a puddle. She skidded into the puddle, and the water formed a geyser that lifted her up as if she were on a pedestal. It twirled her around. "Wheee!" Rani cried.

Prilla clapped her hands. "Rani! Can you make it do that for me?"

"Sure! Come on in," she urged.

Prilla lowered her head and ran splashing into the puddle, just as she had seen Rani do. Rani stretched her arms out to the water. It moved toward her like iron to a magnet. She threw her arms up like a conductor signaling an orchestra.

Voilà! The water created a second geyser that lifted Prilla into the air until she was level with Rani.

Rani laughed. "Now let's seesaw!" The twin water pedestals began to move. Up and down. Up and down. Prilla up. Rani down. Rani up. Prilla down.

Soon both the fairies were laughing so hard, they were in danger of falling off their water pedestals. "Water down," Rani commanded, lowering her arms.

The twin geysers gently subsided. Rani looked down at a shallow puddle spreading out before her feet. She leaned over and grasped the edges of the puddle with her hands. Then she pulled up a sheet of water as if it were a bolt of silvery silk.

She wrapped it around herself like a shimmering cloak. The water gleamed and glittered. It reflected the trees, the sky, and the astonished sparkle in Prilla's eyes.

"How beautiful!" Prilla gasped. "You look like a queen."

Rani held out her hands and quickly caught a raindrop. She held her hands over Prilla's head and let it drip through her fingers. Each droplet was like a tiny diamond. The drops stacked up on Prilla's head and formed a glittering water tiara.

"Now you need a dress to go with that tiara. Water sequins, I think." Rani pulled off her water cape and twirled it in the air. The silky sheet of water broke into a thousand silvery drops. They rained back down on Prilla, clinging to her arms, legs, and torso. Within seconds, Prilla was covered in a sparkling gown of water sequins, complete with a long train.

Prilla took a hesitant step. She expected the watery gown and crown to immediately drip away. But when she moved, they moved with her.

"Rani, you are amazing!" said Prilla. "No wonder you love the water. Believe it or not, I hope it rains again – "

" – tomorrow?" Rani said with a laugh. She had a habit of finishing her friends' sentences for them. "I wish that every day. But rain is rare in Pixie Hollow."

"Wouldn't it be wonderful if you could make it rain whenever – "

" – I wanted? Yes! I can't imagine anything more fun." Rani turned her face up and watched the clouds drift away. It *would* be wonderful to make it rain whenever she wanted. In fact, Rani had been thinking about that for a long time.

Just then, Rani saw a small rain cloud trailing behind the other clouds. Its fluffy edges gleamed silver against the late afternoon sun.

If Rani wanted her own personal rain cloud, that little cloud would be the perfect one. Rani pressed her lips together, thinking.

"I'm getting cold," Prilla said. She shook off her watery finery. "I'm going inside to dry off. I'll see you – "

" – later." Rani waved as Prilla walked back to the Home Tree, where the fairies lived.

Prilla was the only mainland-visiting clapping-talent fairy in Pixie Hollow. In a blink, she could transport herself to the mainland where Clumsies – that is, humans – lived and urge them to clap to show they believed in fairies.

Everyone in Pixie Hollow had been amazed and surprised to discover that Prilla had such an unusual talent. But after a very short time, they stopped being amazed and surprised and took it

very much for granted. After all, why *wouldn'*
a fairy have an unusual talent?

Never Land was an amazing and
surprising place with more kind
of magic than anyone could eve
understand or imagine. But it was thei
talents that made the fairies sc
special. A talent was a kind of magic. And
Rani's water talent seemed tc
be getting stronger and stronger every day
Her relationship to water, and
all things made from it, was becoming mor
personal.

Maybe it was because she couldn't fly
Maybe Rani took all the passion that the
other fairies devoted to their flying and
devoted it instead to her talent.

Rani watched the clouds disappear into
the distance. The smallest one with the

gleaming edges trailed behind. There was something Rani had wanted to try for a long time. Something that would test the power of her talent.

Now, Rani decided boldly. *Now is the time!*

2

RANI RACED UP the spiral stairs inside the trunk of the Home Tree. She ran down the hallway. Her room was located at the very end of one of the longest branches.

Once she was in her room, Rani hurried to the window. She parted the seaweed curtains and peered out.

Rani's room was always damp, which was exactly how she liked it. A permanent leak in the ceiling dripped into a tub made from a human-sized thimble. A Never minnow swam happily in the tub.

Rani listened hard as the water splashed into the thimble. Water spoke a magic language full of dots, plops, plinks, and gurgles. Rani felt as if the water were speaking directly to her. She could hear it encouraging her. It was telling her exactly how to coax the little gray rain cloud back to Pixie Hollow.

Rani fixed her gaze on the cloud and leaned out the window as far as she dared. She stretched out her arms and began to imitate the sounds of the dots, plops, plinks, and gurgles. She called out to the cloud, speaking the language of water.

The little cloud with the shining silver silhouette seemed to pause. Then, drawn by the sound of Rani's voice, it began to move toward her. While the rest of the clouds moved on, little by little the small cloud came drifting back toward the Home Tree.

Rani put every drop of her strength into her water spell. Finally, the cloud hovered right over the branch of the Home Tree where Rani's room was perched.

Exhausted, Rani sank back onto her bed. She listened to the rain patter on the ground outside. She felt the gray watery mist of the cloud come in through the window. It surrounded her like a soft, moist blanket. Her eyelids fluttered, and she fell asleep.

Rani awoke with a start. The sun shone on her face. She found herself looking out the window at a clear blue sky.

"Why! I fell asleep in my clothes," she said.

She pulled the seaweed curtain aside and looked out at the sunny day. There wasn't a rain cloud in sight.

Rani realized that she had been dreaming. She couldn't help feeling disappointed. Having her own little rain cloud would have been wonderful.

She hurried downstairs. As she stepped outside to look for Brother Dove, she heard someone call to her.

"Yoo-hoo! Rani!"

Rani looked up. She saw Prilla waving from the window of her own room in the Home Tree.

Prilla flew out the window and landed lightly on the ground beside Rani. "I had such a good time playing in the rain yesterday. I was almost disappointed when I woke up and saw – "

" – the sun?" Rani finished for her. "Me, too. In fact, you'll laugh when I tell you what I dreamed."

Rani told Prilla all about her dream. Prilla giggled at the idea of Rani having a cloud of her own. "What a shame it turned out to be a dream," she said. "But don't be too disappointed. Sunny days might not be as much fun as rainy days, but they're good for getting things done. What shall we do today?"

As they stood chatting in the soft, yellow morning sunlight, a shadow slowly moved overhead. It blocked out the sun. Moments later, a raindrop splashed down next to them.

Rani looked up and drew in her breath. Hovering overhead was a small gray cloud.

"Prilla! It's the cloud from my dream!" Rani exclaimed.

"It can't be," Prilla said.

"It is!" Rani argued. "I know it. I feel it. It's my very own cloud. Oh, Prilla! It wasn't a dream. I am so lucky!"

Suddenly, Rani heard an odd sound. It sounded like laughter. But it also sounded like water moving through a pipe. "Did you hear that noise?" she asked Prilla.

"I heard a gurgling sound," Prilla replied.

Rani looked down and saw water collecting in a hole next to a root. The water bounced around in the hollow, bubbling and frothing. "I guess that's what we heard." She turned her face up and spread her arms, welcoming the rain. "Just think," she said to Prilla. "Now I can take a walk in the rain every single day, and nobody else has to get wet."

Prilla flew a few feet to the side so she was out of the cloud's shadow. The drizzle fell only on Rani. Prilla laughed. "How perfect. Come on, let's walk to Havendish Stream and see if it follows."

The two fairies began walking toward the stream. All the while, the little rain cloud hovered over Rani and showered her. Some drops plopped on her head, as if the cloud were teasing her and trying to get her to join in a game. Rani broke into a run, trying to escape the drops. The little cloud chased her. It pounded the top of her head with water. Finally, she gave up and slowed down.

Soon Rani and Prilla were laughing so hard they could hardly move. Once again, Rani heard the sound of strange laughter. This time it sounded like water rushing out of a faucet into a copper pot.

Rani began to get an odd feeling. Someone – or something – was watching them. But who? What?

Then suddenly, out of the corner of her eye, Rani saw a figure zip from one flower to another.

Rani pretended not to see. And she didn't say anything to Prilla. She was already planning a way to catch the spy.

"Come on, Prilla," she said in a loud voice. "I'll race you to Havendish Stream." Rani broke into a run. Prilla chased behind her, flying a few inches overhead.

Then, without warning, Rani came to a sudden stop and whirled around.

Prilla shot past her. "Hey!" she cried out in surprise.

Rani kept her eyes focused on one spot. Whoever it was, or whatever it was, froze. It stood perfectly still, hoping to blend into the background. But Rani's eyes were keen. "I see you," she said.

Rani heard a mischievous giggle. It sounded like a bucket splashing down into a well. "If you can see me, I guess there's no point in hiding," the strange creature said. It stepped forward.

Prilla flew over and landed on the ground next to Rani. "What is it?" Prilla whispered.

It looked like a fairy, but it wasn't.

For one thing, it had no wings. In fact, it had no body either. It was a transparent, shimmering figure made of clear water. When it stood still, it was almost invisible. But when it moved, its watery form reflected the sky, the trees, and the flowers.

Rani stared at the remarkable creature. "Who are you? And why are you following us?"

The watery figure laughed. The noise sounded like water splashing in a fountain.

"My name is Dab," the creature said. "I'm a water sprite. And that's my cloud."

Collect all the Disney Fairies books

Discover the story of the Never Fairies in Fairy Dust and the Quest for the Egg